Then Comes Love

a Blue Harbor novel

OLIVIA MILES

Rosewood Press

ALSO BY OLIVIA MILES

Blue Harbor Series
A Place for Us
Second Chance Summer
Because of You
Small Town Christmas
Return to Me

Stand-Alone Titles
Meet Me at Sunset
This Christmas

Oyster Bay Series
Feels Like Home
Along Came You
Maybe This Time
This Thing Called Love
Those Summer Nights
Christmas at the Cottage
Still the One
One Fine Day
Had to Be You

Misty Point Series
One Week to the Wedding
The Winter Wedding Plan

Sweeter in the City Series
Sweeter in the Summer
Sweeter Than Sunshine
No Sweeter Love
One Sweet Christmas

Briar Creek Series
Mistletoe on Main Street
A Match Made on Main Street
Hope Springs on Main Street
Love Blooms on Main Street
Christmas Comes to Main Street

Harlequin Special Edition
'Twas the Week Before Christmas
Recipe for Romance

Then Comes Love

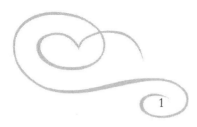

1

Wedding season came to Blue Harbor every year, once the sun grew warmer and the flowers bloomed, and sailboats could be seen bobbing on Lake Huron again. At the official start of each summer, most Saturdays on Gabby Conway's calendar were already circled, and she prided herself on creating unique and personal centerpieces and bouquets for each special day. Every week, it seemed, she watched another blissful bride clutch one of her creations before beginning her march down the aisle, and for a brief moment, Gabby's own heart was full.

And then, every time, she was reminded head-on of what others had found and she hadn't. Yet. Only, as the time went on and the wedding dates were set and more available men were snatched up, she was beginning to wonder if it would ever happen for her.

She sighed as she hung up the phone and circled another Saturday on her calendar, this one not until fall, at least, because most brides did plan months in advance, though there was the occasional impromptu ceremony, which was always a little harried but almost more romantic, in Gabby's opinion. She was receiving more business than usual now that her sister Brooke was back in town and had opened a bridal shop just down the street, and the work was at least keeping her mind off her personal life—or lack thereof. Still, every once in a while, when she made a particularly beautiful bouquet that included her favorite flowers, she couldn't help but think…when? When would it finally happen for her? When would she find true love?

"Let me guess," her mother said as she came around the counter holding a vase of tea roses. "Another wedding?"

"That makes one nearly every weekend through September," Gabby remarked. And it was only June. Her mother had always put in a few hours at the shop each week to help with deliveries or manage orders, but it was still difficult to keep things going at this pace. "I'm afraid I probably won't make it to Summer in the Square this weekend."

The annual town event was something Gabby looked forward to, but she wasn't going to turn her back on business or disappoint a bride. She knew by her mother's expression what she was thinking: that it was high time for Gabby to hire a full-time assistant, at least for the spring and summer seasons. But that would mean handing over control of her creations, and Gabby couldn't help but like her designs the way she envisioned them.

"You know I'm happy to help at the Sunday market to get you through the busy season," her mother replied.

The market at Conway Orchard was a weekly tradition that Gabby looked forward to—especially as her cousins also participated. But with so much to do, and mostly on her own, she wasn't in a position to turn down her mother's help.

"Thanks," she said. "I know I can always count on you."

"You could probably learn to trust someone else if you'd be open to hiring a proper assistant." Her mother arched a brow.

Gabby refused to take the bait. "But you and I have the exact same taste. And the arrangement you just made is proof of that." She grinned broadly, knowing that her mother would cave to the flattery.

"These are lovely, aren't they?" Her mother bent to smell the roses, something that Gabby still did every time she made an arrangement. It was important to appreciate the small things, the reason she had opened this business to begin with, and, of course, to know that she was only giving her customers the very best.

"They are." Gabby herself was a fan of these pale pink roses, more of a blush color in hue than some of the other variations she carried. They were just as lovely and soft in a mixed bouquet as they were on their own. "Nothing beats a classic," she said now, as she often did.

Still, creatively speaking, she was always excited when it was time to create a mixed bouquet. Keeping up with the trends was important in this business, as was staying one step ahead of the brides when it came to big ideas.

She sighed as she looked up to see one coming in now.

The bell above the door jingled as her Uncle Dennis's fiancée approached the counter. Candy was dressed in head-to-toe pink, her favorite color, and Gabby felt weary knowing that with Candy and Dennis's wedding now only four weeks away, there was little time for Candy to change her mind about the flowers.

Again.

"I just came from my dress fitting!" Candy's smile was radiant as her eyes flicked over the room, landing on a birthday bouquet that Gabby had set aside for pickup.

Oh, no. No distractions. No temptation. No room for doubt. In the months since getting engaged, Candy had changed her mind about her flowers at least six times, and Gabby knew that Brooke had to tweak her wedding dress design at least as much. If not more.

"How was it?" Gabby and her mother exchanged a subtle glance. No doubt the next person through the door would be Brooke, needing to vent.

Some days Gabby didn't know who was looking forward to Candy and Dennis's wedding the most. The Conway girls or the bride herself.

"Lovely, lovely! Just perfect!"

Gabby felt her shoulders relax until she sensed a pause.

"Just a few minor tweaks," Candy continued with a smile.

Gabby held her breath, knowing that the dress was separate from the flowers, and of course, everything looked different on the hanger. She smiled reassuringly and said, "I'm sure that it will be perfect, no matter what."

"Now, you're probably thinking that I'm here to discuss the flowers," Candy said.

Gabby's heart skipped a beat. "Actually, I think I've got all the information I need. All that's left is the sample bouquet."

Candy's eyes flicked to the roses that Gabby's mother held. "Those are lovely, Miriam. So sweet and dainty. And pink. Oh, I feel like I'm describing myself!" She laughed loudly, and Gabby had to bite her lip. Candy could be sweet, and she did love pink, but she was not what anyone would describe as dainty, neither in stature nor in personality. "Gabby, I don't recall seeing this variety of rose last time I was here."

Which had been about four days ago…

Gabby watched her mother bite her lip and mutter something about limited stock. With a knowing glance at Gabby, she then quickly set the arrangement on the workbench behind the counter, away from Candy's prying eyes.

"What can I help you with today then?" Gabby didn't have the energy to think about another design concept just now, and she wasn't surprised that Candy would have changes for her so soon, either. It was one of the reasons she had held off on the sample bouquet. While normally she assembled a scaled-down version of the final design weeks in advance, this part of the process was meant to only give the bride a visual, and usually only included a discussion about adding a ribbon or removing one variety of flower. But Candy put even the highest maintenance of brides to shame, and the less time Candy had to doubt herself again the better.

"Well, I was going over the guest list," Candy said, pulling what Gabby had come to recognize as her "wedding binder" (pink, of course) from her oversized handbag. "And I see that you have only RSVP'd with one."

As if she needed the reminder. Gabby nodded. "That's right. Singles table." But at least she'd be in good company with her sister Jenna at her side, along with a few of her cousins on her mother's side of the family, who had always been embraced by the Conways.

"I just wanted to let you know that if you would like to bring Jackson Bradford as your plus one, I can seat you two at a different table..." Candy blinked at her so earnestly that Gabby burst out laughing.

"Why does everyone in this town think I have something going on with Jackson?" Sure, the man was attractive, but he was also a complete cad. As the bartender of the popular pub at the Carriage House Inn, he was in his element flashing smiles, pouring drinks, and chatting with the ladies. Jackson was fun, but she was looking for...well, forever.

"It's just that you two would make *such* beautiful babies," Candy lamented, and now it was Gabby's mother's turn to laugh.

"Candy," she said, stepping forward to take over the situation. "While I agree that Gabby and Jackson might make a beautiful couple, I think that it's best to let Gabby's heart find its own path. As longstanding family friends, all the Bradfords will be at the wedding anyway. No need to push things."

Candy pushed her lips together. She had considered herself something of a local matchmaker in recent months, meddling in her future stepdaughters' love lives to her own heart's content. Granted, now all of Gabby's cousins on her father's side were happily settled into relationships, whereas Gabby...

Gabby was at the singles table.

"I was just about to deliver this lovely arrangement to Helena over at the library. She's hosting a small event today for the benefactors and I don't want this centerpiece for the refreshments table to be late." Gabby's mother lifted the vase of tea roses again and came around the counter. "I'll walk you out," she said to Candy, in a way that was friendly but firm enough to leave no room for argument.

Candy looked back at Gabby with a disappointed sigh. "If you change your mind…"

"I won't," Gabby said pleasantly. "But thank you."

She chuckled to herself as her mother and future aunt finally left the store, the door closing behind them, leaving her in peace. She finished clipping the stems of the snapdragons and placed them in a bucket of water, then went to the sink to rinse her shears. There was an entire bucket of yellow roses to de-thorn and clip, and she reached for the first one, stopping to smell it first. She smiled, as she always did, because it never got old. What did get old was that the only man who had sent her flowers in her entire lifetime was her father, bless his heart.

She carefully set the first rose in a bucket she'd filled with fresh water when the door chimed again.

She glanced up, only mildly surprised to see that it was a man. Usually, the men called orders in over the phone, but some of the older gents in town still stopped in to pick out something personally, and she loved them for it. Chivalry was sadly a dying practice, at least in her world.

But here, she noticed, as she perked up a bit, was a tall, broad-shouldered man with sandy brown hair, and a thick head of it from the looks of it. She swallowed hard, her

eyes immediately darting to the left hand that was now reaching out to tap—yes, tap—the petals of a gerbera daisy, before letting it drop.

God help her, it was bare.

Still, he was in a flower shop. Meaning, he obviously had someone special in his life.

"Those are new this week," she said cheerfully, painfully aware that it was just the two of them in the store and that her mother could be back at any moment for the next delivery, very possibly with Candy still nipping at her heels.

"They're so perfect, for a moment I thought they were fake." The man turned to give her a smile.

Fake flowers in her shop? She nearly laughed, if she wasn't so surprised to see that the man was none other than Doug Monroe.

She stiffened impulsively, then forced her composure. This was a place of business, and more importantly, it was her place of business, and besides, she hadn't seen Doug Monroe since high school graduation. She'd been pleased about it at the time. The guy had been a proverbial thorn in her side for the better half of her teenage years, first when they were paired against each other in debate and he had gone and insulted her stance on whether the cafeteria should ban chocolate milk, and later, when they'd run against each other for senior class president…and she'd lost. But the worst of it had been the prom planning committee, something he'd joined both junior and senior year, claiming it looked good on college applications, even after he'd already been accepted to Notre Dame.

But the Doug she knew back in high school was tall and lanky, with tortoise-rimmed glasses that made it hard to read his eyes, whereas the man that stood before her was…well. Not like how she remembered him at all.

She was suddenly aware that she was staring.

"Doug?" She smiled warmly. Surely if his physical appearance proved anything, it was that he had changed from the unfriendly teenager to a well-adjusted man, who didn't appear to be married.

"Gabby Conway." He grinned, and for a moment, she relaxed. She was just being silly, judging him based on his behavior back in school. That was well over a decade ago now. "Do you own this shop?"

She nodded. Every inch of this place was her pride and joy. Not a detail had been overlooked, from the soft honey-colored paint that was the perfect backdrop to any flower, to the blue and white striped awning under the shop sign, to the little cardstock labels she affixed to the buckets with twine, that not only identified each flower but also gave her personal thoughts on what made it so special.

Then she remembered that he had planned on going to law school after Notre Dame, something he had been quite sure to mention during his nauseating campaign speeches at the start of senior year. He'd done just that because if Doug was anything, he was a man with a plan.

This shop probably didn't seem like much of an accomplishment by comparison, and her old competitive spirit flared.

"Are you visiting?" she asked with a smile. No need to hold a grudge, after all, even if she had looked forward to the prom planning committee since she'd first heard of it freshman year, and had filled a sketchbook with ideas that he seemed to question every chance he had.

He shook his head. "Nah, I moved back a few weeks ago, actually."

Moved back? Her mouth went dry. Blue Harbor offered many things, but eligible bachelors were not one of them, especially when Gabby factored in how many of the men in town had dated one of her cousins or sisters or friends—making them officially off-limits. The list had dwindled to, well, Jackson Bradford. Maybe, at a stretch, Ryan Harrison, also known as her sister Brooke's brother-in-law, so that got a little weird. Only now, it seemed like there may be a fresh face, or if not fresh, distantly familiar.

She'd settle on fresh. Enough time had passed for a second chance.

"Wow," she said, somehow finding the words. "That's a big change. You were in Cleveland, right?" It wasn't that she was interested, more like word traveled in a town as small as Blue Harbor. Though there had been no mention of return.

"Columbus," he said, his smile dropping a bit.

Well, enough pleasantries. It was clear he wasn't going to elaborate, and what did she care why he left the city? He was back in Blue Harbor. Back to stay from the sounds of it. And he was obviously in her shop for a reason.

Gabby snagged an order form from her counter. "What can I do for you today?"

"My father called in an order. He asked me to pick it up for him."

"Of course!" Gabby beamed. She'd been so distracted by those deep-set eyes that she'd never noticed before to even connect him with the order she'd filled earlier. "Your father is such a sweetheart, always sending your mother flowers on her birthday."

Doug raised his eyebrows. "Can't see why. They just die within days."

Her eyes narrowed slightly. Still, she forced herself to remain positive. "With proper care, they can last longer, and of course, flowers are the simplest expression of love, if you ask me." Which he hadn't. And she'd just said the word love. And now he was looking at her like she had a third eye.

"I mean, once you know someone's favorite flower, it's such an intimate, personal gift." She felt her cheeks flush. Intimate? There would be hell to pay if her sisters or cousins ever caught wind of this. It was just like Doug to get her all tongue-tied and flustered, something he seemed to take endless joy in doing when they stood at their posts in debate club. Of course, she had only joined because she'd had eyes for Chad Johnson, captain of the soccer team, who was only on the debate team for extra credit due to his shaky grades. And much as she'd tried to catch his attention, the only one who seemed determined to jostle her was Doug.

His gaze was steady on hers. "What's your favorite flower?"

She smiled at this. Finally, something she could say without any room for stumbling over her words. "That's easy. A Juliet rose. Roses are classic, timeless really. I guess you could say that I'm a hopeless romantic."

She felt her eyes widen on her misstep. She had even managed to botch that response!

"Well." She cleared her throat. "Let me just get that arrangement for you." She hurried to the arrangement that she'd set aside. It was a colorful mix of garden roses, peonies, snapdragons, blue thistle, and ranunculus, and she was quite proud to present it and show what she was capable of creating. Certainly, he would need no further convincing.

But as she picked it up and presented it to him, Doug just said, "How much do I owe you?"

She exhaled nervously and flicked through her order sheets until she found the one that had been called in that morning. "That will be fifty, even."

"Fifty dollars!" Now Doug was laughing, pretty good and hard, and Gabby had the uneasy feeling that it was at her expense. "And I thought my rates were high!"

Ah, yes, the one-upmanship. So it would seem not much had changed since high school after all.

"Fresh flowers of this quality are not free," she assured him, lest he think she was running some kind of racket.

Instead, he motioned to the door and said, "Plenty of them growing for free on most people's front yards."

She pinched her lips, not bothering to point out that those flowers would most certainly die within a few days, if not hours, and she highly doubted that he was growing blue thistle in *his* front landscaping, let alone snapdragons, peonies, and... Oh, she was getting worked up again.

"Well, I think it's a lovely gesture on your father's part." She felt very defensive of Mr. Monroe, who was a loyal customer, and, clearly, a devoted husband to dear Carol. Too bad the same couldn't be said for their son, Gabby thought with a sniff.

"Could have bought her a bracelet for this amount." Doug shook his head as he pulled out his credit card. "Would have lasted longer."

"And been quite impersonal," Gabby clipped. She swiped the card quickly and eyed the machine, suddenly keen to get him on his way and out of her store. He wasn't just bad for business. He was bad for morale. "Besides, not everything is meant to last forever. Some things are meant to be enjoyed for the small amount of time they are with us."

"Ah, so you admit that your product has a short shelf life." His grin was one of amusement, or perhaps victory, she could never be sure.

Gabby felt her nostrils flare, and she handed him back the card along with the receipt. She knew better than to expect a tip and was almost miffed when he stuffed some bills in the jar.

"I hope your mother enjoys them," she managed, because she sincerely did. She put her heart into every bouquet, and once she got to know a client's tastes and preferences, she was able to truly perfect their arrangements. This year, she had a clear winner for Carol Monroe, regardless of what Doug might think.

Doug said nothing to affirm that she would, but just held up his hand and said, "It was nice seeing you, Gabby. Feels like old times."

Gabby felt her smile whither as she watched him go and then plucked a rose from the bucket, accidentally popping the head from the stem in her haste. If by old times he meant sparring off on every topic from trade wars with foreign countries to whether they should go with colored or clear lights for the winter wonderland prom theme, he was right.

But she'd be damned if she'd let him have the final word when it came to romance.

2

Gabby waited until her mother had returned to take her lunch break, even if she had lost her appetite. Honestly! The nerve of that man! To not only insult her store, but to undermine her passion and cheapen the mere notion of romance?

Her funk must have been noticeable by the time she arrived at the door of Something Blue, her middle sister's bridal shop. Because she knew that her scowl was probably bad for business, and because she honestly couldn't face yet another blushing bride-to-be just now, she peeked through the window before pushing through the door, relieved to see Brooke come from the back room alone, her arms laden with frothy tulle.

"Hey!" Brooke said brightly. "Just in time. Mind helping me hang these veils?"

Gabby felt a literal pang when she reached for the one on top. Three layers of soft, white tulle hanging from a sparkling crystal band.

"You want to try it on, don't you?" Brooke's grin was cheeky.

Was it so obvious? Sure, she had indulged before, probably more often than she should, really. But today Gabby shook her head. "There's no point. I'll never get married at this rate."

"Oh, now, what happened to that hopeless romantic sister of mine?"

Gabby draped the veil over the satin hanger and set it on the hook Brooke indicated. Her eyes swept the room; she couldn't help herself. The entire boutique was like an adult candy store for the lonely hearts in town. And right now, she felt like she was at the top of the list. It was bad enough that she was the eldest sister and that Brooke was already married. Oh, it was nothing new of course. Brooke had been married years ago, to her teenage sweetheart. Meanwhile, Gabby had never even had a date to the prom—that she'd helped to plan.

A foreshadowing of things to come, she thought darkly.

"I'll tell you what happened," Gabby said. "I've realized that being a romantic is exactly what you said. Hopeless."

Brooke was having none of it. She gave a little smile and motioned Gabby to the seating area in the center of the room. On the marble coffee table was Brooke's lookbook, similar to the one Gabby had back at Sweet Stems—a brag book, essentially, full of photographs of their best work; only in Gabby's shop, customers came around the counter. There was no velvet seating in her shop. No ball gowns either, she thought, letting her attention drift to the corner of the room where one of Brooke's newest designs was on full display.

"Your mouth says one thing, but your face says another." Brooke's expression was rueful when Gabby finally looked away from the soft and lovely and oh so romantic creation. "What happened?"

Gabby sucked in a breath, not sure if she wanted to bother with the details of her morning, but instead settled on the bigger issue. "I have a wedding every month through September."

"So do I," Brooke said. "Not that I'm complaining. Business has been better than I could have hoped, with a little help from you, of course."

Gabby managed a smile. It was true that as sisters and fellow shop owners who both catered to the bridal industry, they were able to cross-promote, or at least send a client in each other's direction. Though some of those clients they probably preferred to have never met.

"Candy was in today," Gabby said drolly.

Brooke rolled her eyes to the ceiling. "She was here, too. Now she wants to shorten the train! Well, little does she know that I'm not doing it. Knowing Candy, she'd change her mind and want it longer at the last minute, and it's much different to add fabric than it is to take it away."

Gabby laughed. "You sound like me. I already told her the sample bouquet won't be ready until the day before her wedding. I usually do that weeks in advance."

"At least she can use it for her rehearsal," Brooke pointed out.

True. Her sister was smart, and not just in business. She'd picked the right guy years ago, even if she hadn't exactly found eternal bliss with him until recently when she'd moved back to town and opened her shop. Like Gabby,

Brooke prided herself on her creative energy, but unlike Gabby, Brooke had managed to find a personal life too.

"She was trying to push me to invite Jackson to the wedding as my date, even though he's already invited, of course." Gabby sighed, and Brooke could only laugh. Not only was this classic Candy, but Brooke knew Gabby well enough to be sure that Jackson was not long-term relationship material.

Maybe no one was. With a wedding every weekend between now and Labor Day, the single men were quickly being snatched up, for good.

"I suppose that I should be grateful for a free glass of champagne after a long day," Gabby said, thinking of the wedding she had tomorrow, down at the Yacht Club, a popular destination in town for such things. She usually got to know her brides so well, they were all too kind to invite her to stay and enjoy their big day, even if, lately, she wished they wouldn't.

"A reward for your efforts! Look at it like that." Brooke reached over and squeezed her hand. "Besides, you love a good wedding as much as you love one of those paperback romance novels you read by the dozen."

Gabby went quiet. It was true that once she loved standing behind the guests, watching from a professional distance as the bride began her wedding march, and later, her eyes would mist as the happy couple took their first official dance as man and wife, but something had shifted, and this morning hadn't helped matters. She'd dared to hope, but now, that hope was starting to fade.

"I'm nearly in my mid-thirties," she said bluntly.

"So?" Brooke straightened the items on her coffee table.

"And Blue Harbor isn't exactly crawling with men."

"Hasn't stopped me," Brooke replied. "Or most of our cousins."

"Are you saying that there is something wrong with me?" Gabby wasn't insulted, and this sisterly banter wasn't new either. They'd had this conversation hundreds of times through their teen years when Gabby was always single and Brooke was happily dating Kyle Harrison. She knew exactly what Brooke would say before she even opened her mouth. Sometimes, she needed to hear it, though.

"I've said it before, and I'll say it again. I think you could stand to be just a little less picky," Brooke said pertly.

"And date Jackson Bradford?" Last Gabby had checked, the man didn't date, at least, not for long.

"Not Jackson," Brooke said to her relief. "But maybe, keep your heart open."

"My heart is open!" Gabby cried, sitting up straighter. Or at least, it had been. So she thought.

"For something less than perfect?" Brooke raised an eyebrow.

"What's wrong with holding out for true love?" Gabby retorted. "Are you suggesting I lower my standards?" Settling down was one thing, but settling? She couldn't imagine anything worse.

"I just think that relationships take work and compromise…"

"I've never really had a long-term relationship, as you may recall," Gabby reminded her sister. The sad truth was

that she wasn't even often asked out on dates. Sure, there had been a few setups over the years, a few casual weeks with tourists or summer staff. "And now I don't even have a date to these weddings."

"Maybe that's a good thing," Brooke said.

Gabby perked up a bit. "It's true that the singles table are where the eligible men would be…"

Brooke swatted her. "I mean, take some pressure off yourself. Go to the weddings, have some fun. Be yourself. Go for a good time, not to look for your soulmate."

Be herself. It was so seldom that she met a man that checked her boxes, that Gabby wasn't sure she could trust herself to be anything less than her best self, meaning she squared her shoulders, smiled her best smile, and was, well, basically a stiffer version of the Gabby she let her friends and family see.

Brooke hesitated. "Just…don't be too quick to judge."

Gabby let that sink in for a minute. Too quick to judge she could work with—unless, of course, the evidence was glaring.

*

Doug pulled up to a stop behind his brother's SUV, taking in the old, wood-sided house that he'd called home every one of his thirty-three years. Columbus had never been home, and he'd just been unable to realize that at the time. Too blinded by love.

Too fooled, really.

It wasn't a large home; if anything, it was one of the smallest in Blue Harbor, but his mother took pride in it and always had: flowers bloomed in the window boxes, the yard was a vibrant green, and the interior always felt like it was waiting for company to stop over at any moment. Doug carried the flowers carefully, a little surprised that they hadn't yet wilted, and let himself in the front door, where his father met him in the hall. "Ah, thanks for doing that for me, son. One of the perks of having you back, eh?"

Doug sniffed the air, and his stomach grumbled from the aroma. "One of many," he said, thinking of the endless supply of frozen pizza, take-out, and restaurant fare he'd lived on for most of his adult life. His ex, Lisa, had never been much of a cook, and neither was he. His father, on the other hand…

"Let me guess?" He hesitated, trying to discern the scent, until he settled on the obvious. "Paella?"

"Your mother's favorite," his father said with a smile of contentment.

Doug followed his father down the hall to the dining room, where his mother was already seated at the head of the table, Doug's brother Justin to her left, in his childhood chair.

Carol's face broke out into a smile as she stood to collect the arrangement. "Oh, Doug! You spoil me so!"

"Something beautiful for my beautiful birthday girl," Doug's father replied, looking downright proud as his wife set the vase in the center of the table.

Doug and Justin exchanged a glance. Growing up, they'd been embarrassed by their parents' affection. Thought it was downright corny. Now, Doug had to admit it was sort of sweet.

27

But there was another feeling there too, one that hadn't been there before, one that didn't even really make sense. If he didn't know better, he might call it jealousy.

"Happy birthday, Mom," he said, shaking away those thoughts and leaning down to kiss his mother on the cheek. He handed over the small gift he'd purchased that morning. "And here's my gift. It's a gift card to the salon," he explained as she opened the envelope. "I thought you could treat yourself one of these afternoons."

"Oh. How…thoughtful." His mother's eyes crinkled into a smile, but it wasn't as big as the one she'd given him when she'd thought he'd been responsible for the flowers. He had half a mind to show her the size of the voucher— enough for a full day of pampering and spa treatments, but his mother patted his hand and said, "Would you mind helping your father with dinner? Every time I stand up, he orders me back into my chair." She laughed, and he nodded.

"Sure thing, Mom." He noticed the card from his father propped on the buffet table next to what was clearly a homemade cake. While an expert on the range, baking was one of Howard's newer endeavors, and his decorating skills had a long way to go.

"Hey, Dad," he said, coming into the kitchen where the counters were piled high with empty boxes and cutting boards, cutlery, and evidence of a lot of work. "I could have picked up a cake at the grocery store for you, too, you know."

"A cake from the grocery store?" His father nearly laughed.

"Or the bakery..." Doug had noticed a new one in town since his last visit. Buttercream Bakery, owned by one of the Conway girls, apparently.

Conway. His mind drifted to Gabby Conway. Always the prettiest of that family, if anyone were to ask him, not that it was really debatable. Gabby Conway had the most beautiful smile, the shiniest hair, the brightest eyes, and the most difficult personality of all her sisters and cousins combined. She knew what she wanted and she didn't back down, and he'd seen that firsthand on those disastrous prom planning committees he'd signed up for as a way to stay involved in school activities. Don't bother asking her for a date, so the locker room talk would go. Gabby was very pretty, and like many pretty girls, she knew it. And most guys weren't looking to set themselves up for rejection.

Doug sure wasn't. Ever again.

"I know my cake might not be a looker, but it's your mother's birthday," Howard continued. "It's my day to spoil her. And as the saying goes, it's the thought that counts."

That was a common phrase in their house, especially during the years where his father's business took a hit. Before he retired, Doug's father owned a boating and water sports rental company, which heavily depended on tourists, as did most businesses in Blue Harbor. When the rains were heavy, or the weather too cool, Howard felt the sting. There were many homemade gifts those years, Doug remembered. It was one of the reasons he'd always promised himself to see that those holidays didn't happen again. That his parents would be secure. That they wouldn't need to worry about their business, or him. He'd helped out free of charge once he was old enough, maintained strong enough grades to get a full ride to college and then law school.

He'd never given his parents cause for worry. Until now, it would seem.

Looking around the mess of the kitchen, Doug understood why his father kept ordering his mother back into her chair every time she stood up. She'd be trapped in that seat until midnight if Doug or Justin didn't roll up their sleeves and pitch in.

"Let me at least get a start on these dishes while you finish up," he said to his father.

"Now that is an offer I won't argue with." Howard laughed.

Doug made some headway on the counter and loaded up the dishwasher by the time his father had transferred the paella to a large serving bowl. Doug grabbed two bottles of wine—one white, one red—and carried them into the dining room, just in time to hear the tail end of a conversation that was unabashedly about his true reasons for coming back.

Or at least, part of them. Still, he knew that if he and Lisa had stayed together—if their four-year relationship hadn't come to an abrupt end—he probably wouldn't have been so willing to pack up his belongings and move back to his hometown.

Silver linings, he told himself. Or fate. Either way, the message was clear. He was single, and he was staying that way.

"We're just worried about you," his mother said, reaching out to squeeze his hand.

"Nothing to be worried about here." He forced a smile as he uncorked the first bottle. "I'm happy to be back. When was the last time I got to spend your birthday with you like this?"

Too long, that much was true. He came back at least once a year, usually around the holidays, sent lavish gifts when he couldn't, but there was always his work to keep him busy, and his paid vacation days usually went towards just that—vacation. He'd thought they'd had fun, he and Lisa, on their ski trips and beach getaways. Had the fun just ended, or had it never been there at all?

He swallowed hard, thinking of the final conversation he'd had with Lisa when she'd made everything so shockingly clear that there was no room for conversation. Nothing to do but walk away. Or in his case, move away.

"Besides," he said, jutting his chin at his kid brother. "I haven't heard anything exciting about your love life in a while."

His brother just shook his head. Like Doug, he'd been quiet in school, focused on his studies, but he was also shyer by nature and somehow that gave him a free pass when it came to conversations like this. Besides, he hadn't just ended an engagement either. Doug supposed it was inevitable. It was a hot topic. Eventually, it would fade away, and sooner rather than later.

"At least I'll have someone joining me at the singles table tomorrow," Justin said, helping himself to a glass of Cabernet. Their mother poured white wine for herself.

Doug stifled a groan. He'd nearly forgotten about the wedding he'd agreed to attend tomorrow. Was it late June already? Strange to think he'd been back in town a full month now. In some ways, it felt like he'd just returned, and in other ways, like he'd never left.

"Now don't groan," his mother said, as she spooned some of the rice onto her plate. "You always loved weddings. And the Donaldsons were such nice people. You boys looked forward to them renting out the cottage down the street every single summer. Of course, I did always think it might be one of you who ended up with their daughter, but… Well."

Doug and Justin exchanged a glance. "I'm not much of a wedding person these days."

"Shame. I seem to remember you looking so forward to my brother William's wedding…"

"When I was eight," Doug replied, remembering his uncle's reception, where he'd first discovered the joy of a DJ and a dance floor. Now the thought of dancing appealed to him about as much as the thought of the singles table.

"Well, don't get mad, but when I knew you were coming home, I RSVP'd for all of us to attend the Yates wedding next weekend." She paused when she caught the sharp look he gave her. "They've been our neighbors for all our married life. You boys used to go swimming with Anthony! Besides, we were all on the invitation."

"What am I, twelve?" He shook his head. He should have known that this was what came with returning to his hometown.

"They were just being inclusive," his mother insisted. "And invitations are expensive. The bride's family is paying, and I know they're on a budget."

Yes, invitations were expensive, and he knew that from firsthand experience.

"Fine," he said, seeing little room for argument. That would make three weddings in a row when he factored in the client who had invited him to his nuptials two weeks from now. He was hardly in a position to say no, especially when he was trying to build his law practice in this town from scratch.

"And keep your calendar open for three weeks from tomorrow."

Make that four weddings in a row. "Who is it this time?"

Across the table, he heard Justin laugh, but his mother just pressed her lips together. "You remember my friend Dorothy. It's her youngest's day—her last wedding. How could we say no?"

Dorothy had been an old childhood friend of his mother's, Doug knew. There would be no getting out of this one.

His mother gave a little smile. "Maybe you'll be surprised. You might end up having a better time than you think."

More like he might meet someone, at least that was what her eyes were telling him.

Doug took a long sip from his wineglass. He'd had enough surprises for one year, if not a lifetime, and if his mother was insinuating that he might settle down, or even start dating any time soon, she was sorely mistaken. If it wasn't her birthday he'd tell her so, too, but seeing as it was, he let it pass, along with the weddings he'd be attending tomorrow and next Saturday, and the Saturday after that. And…oh, he couldn't even think about it.

His mother's heart was in the right place, he knew. Always was. She wanted him to be happy. She just didn't realize that he was happier alone.

Or, at least, less disappointed.

He looked over at his mother, who still held his father's hand, and for a moment, he dared to want what they had, to even believe that it was possible.

He shook that thought off right away. He knew from firsthand experience that what his parents had was rare, and that he had not been lucky enough to find it.

3

The Donaldson wedding reception was being held at the Yacht Club, a long-time favorite amongst brides in the county because of its waterfront location and elegant amenities, not to mention the quintessential wood-sided building and lush landscaping. It was also on Gabby's short-list for whenever her big day finally rolled around.

Make that *if* it ever rolled around. Catching her souring mood before it got the better of her, Gabby set the last centerpiece at the head table and stepped back to admire the space under the tent that had been set up right along the water's edge, making sure that each round table was anchored with an antique vase overflowing with lavender, peonies, and roses in soft purple, cream, and pink.

She sighed because she just couldn't help herself. This was a perfectly romantic wedding in the most traditional sense. The bride's bouquet was bound by a simple ivory velvet ribbon, and Gabby had hung a cone of lavender from each church pew earlier in the day. The reception tables were draped in ivory clothes, and the gilded chairs were the perfect complement to the vases.

In the distance, she heard the ringing of the bells, and the cheer that went up as no doubt the newly official bride and groom emerged from the double doors to be greeted by their guests.

She felt her eyes mist just imagining the thrill of that moment, the gauzy veil trailing behind her, catching in the wind as she stopped to kiss her husband on the church steps. She blinked, forcing herself to the present. She was getting swept away, just like Brooke had accused her of doing. Maybe she did read too many romance novels. It was just that lately, they were the only place she seemed to find any romance.

Quickly, she turned the centerpiece on the head table for optimal display. She was not a true guest at this wedding, much less the bride. She was the florist, and right now she estimated that she had about fifteen minutes before people made their way over to the reception, eager for a glass of cold champagne.

She could certainly do with one herself, but not right now. Right now, she needed to make her rounds, ensure that everything was accounted for, so that the bride was just as thrilled walking into the tent as she had been when she'd walked down the aisle.

Her mother had helped out with the earlier part of the day—dropping off the bouquets and boutonnieres for the wedding party, and getting a start on the reception while Gabby finished decorating the church. But now Gabby was down to the final touches, and she'd sent her mother home to relax—not because she couldn't have used the extra hands, but because she enjoyed keeping this task to herself.

She walked a perimeter around the grounds, keeping an eye out for a stray leaf or limp bloom, stopping here and there to give the petals a quick spritz. The guests were starting to arrive. She knew from experience that they'd enjoy the cocktail reception while the bridal party was busy with the photographers, probably on the dock with the lake behind them, Evening Island visible in the distance. Gabby always dressed for the event while she set up, so she would blend in if anyone arrived early. Today had been warm, not a cloud could be seen in the blue sky that would soon enough start to change into a glorious sunset, and even though the lake effect could stir up a cool breeze when you least expected it, she was pleasantly warm in her grass green shift dress.

She stepped back from the last arrangement she had shifted three inches to the right and rotated by forty-five degrees, her heel catching on something that made her nearly lose her footing.

"Woah, there," a deep voice rumbled directly behind her as a hand met her elbow.

Gabby turned to see none other than Doug Monroe, standing right behind her, his dark eyes gleaming as they locked with hers.

She pressed her lips together and stepped away. "I didn't see you there."

Because if she had, she would have run. Or at least speed-walked away. So this was what she got for caring too much about her arrangements. Another tête-à-tête with the local know-it-all.

"I didn't realize that was you," he was sure to say.

Something he didn't know? She was surprised he'd so casually admit it!

He held up a place card, saying ruefully. "Table twelve it is. You?"

Here she breathed a sigh of relief. "I'm just the florist," she said tightly, sure to accentuate the word just to make sure he understood where she stood with his comments yesterday.

"You're not staying?" His eyebrows shot up in a way that made her wonder if he was truly disappointed by this. Or just curious.

She looked around the tent. Even though Blue Harbor was small, she didn't know many of the guests personally. She could duck out after the cocktail hour, drive home, slip off her uncomfortable shoes and dress, and settle onto her sofa with a good book and a cold glass of wine. She had only three chapters left in her latest novel, and despite knowing that it would end happily, she wanted to see just how the heroine reached that point.

Maybe, she could find a few pointers. Or hope, she thought, feeling her shoulders sink a little as she looked over at Doug, who seemed to be frowning now as he studied the name cards at his table.

"Singles table?" she asked with knowing dread.

"At least my brother is with me." Doug picked up a card and studied it. "Though not beside me."

He picked up another card and swapped it out. Gabby felt her jaw slip and she couldn't stop herself from saying, "You can't do that!"

He looked at her frankly. "Why not?"

"Well, well, because the bride put thought into that," Gabby finally said. And it was the bride's day.

But Doug just brushed off her concern with a wave. "I don't think who is sitting beside who at table twelve will be forefront on her mind tonight."

True. And Gabby supposed that people swapped places all the time to avoid awkward setups or conversations with nosy relatives. Now she stepped toward him, hoping for a peek of the cards, wondering just what Doug was avoiding. Or whom he was trying to get closer to.

"And who is that you're hoping to sit next to tonight?" she asked.

"You." His eyes glimmered.

She pursed her lips. Sometimes she was seated with the wedding coordinator and photographers, who barely had time to sit, much less eat a hot meal. It was a courtesy, the table usually being at the back of the room, but with the brides that she grew to know over time, they liked to make her a proper guest, even if she always felt a sense of duty to them until she was sure that every petal was fresh and perfectly displayed.

She eyed the empty place card holder, knowing that Doug was watching her, wondering if she'd dare to commit the crime she'd just accused him of, and switch things around to her comfort zone.

Instead, she forced herself to remember her professional reason for being here, and her polite and handy excuse to leave early. With a faint smile that she hoped masked the tension she felt, she tucked the square of cardstock into its clip and, for lack of anything else to do, accepted a glass of white wine from a waiter.

There was no denying the wicked grin that passed over Doug's face when he did the same.

"You look rather pleased with yourself," she noted. "Enjoying yourself then?"

"I'd rather be home. No offense," he added quickly.

None taken, at least not coming from the source. Gabby frowned at him, wondering if he meant that. Sure, she was already a little tired just thinking about wedding season, but it was also difficult not to be swept away by the music and the decorations and the festive buzz of the guests.

"You'd rather be home alone than outside on this beautiful day, with free drinks, good food, and…" She stopped herself, realizing that she was nearly guilty of the very thing she was accusing him of.

"Weddings aren't my thing," he said.

"Well, they are definitely mine." She laughed under her breath. They were her bread and butter, really, other than Valentine's Day, which unfortunately only came once a year.

"You made all these?" He motioned around the tent, which was starting to fill up as the band began to play. More people were taking their seats, and with any luck, their table would fill soon and they'd be interrupted.

"That's my job," Gabby said, noticing the defensive edge in her tone.

He must have picked up on it, too, because he leaned forward, close enough for her to see the laugh lines around his eyes that made him almost seem likable. "My mother loved the arrangement you made."

Possibly, he was just flattering her, but still, she couldn't resist the smile that pulled at her mouth. It had been a beautiful bouquet.

"It was the center of our dinner table," he added. "She said that all of her favorites were in there."

There was no pushing back the swell in her chest. "It's why I love what I do. There's nothing better than being in the business of putting a smile on someone's face when they need it the most. That part never gets old."

He gave her a funny look and then lifted his eyebrows. "I never thought of it that way."

She wasn't surprised. Still, she was pleased to see he didn't try to argue her point. Instead, he just grinned and said, "My mother was certainly smiling, and that was, well, it was nice to see."

"Oh, I can't completely take credit for that," Gabby said, feeling her shoulders relax a bit. "Your dad pays close attention to what pleases your mother, and he knows what brings her joy. It's so sweet to see people still in love after so many years of marriage."

She sighed, even though she saw Doug's mouth thin.

"You don't agree?" she asked, tipping her head.

He looked over at the bride and groom, who were making their way into the reception, trailed by the wedding photographer.

"Sweet, sure. But…it's rare."

Gabby let out a laugh of surprise, even though it wasn't the least bit funny. "Don't let anyone else hear you say that. It's bad luck at a wedding."

"Well, they'll need luck if they expect to last as long as my parents," Doug continued.

Now Gabby's eyes widened as she looked around, hoping that no one had overheard. "My, aren't you cynical!"

"Not cynical," he replied with an infuriating little shrug. "Just realistic."

She firmed her mouth closed, unsure of what to even say to that. Was it so unrealistic to think that people could fall in love, share a life together, one that they'd look back on in their aging years, reliving memories and moments that no one else could?

"Well, with that attitude, I suppose I shouldn't be surprised that you're sitting at the singles table," she said haughtily.

"I suppose I'll be sitting at one for the rest of my life," Doug commented.

Of course. She should have known. "A confirmed bachelor then?"

She didn't know why she felt disappointed. Probably because this was why she was always at the singles table. All the good men were taken, and the rest were...confirmed bachelors.

And even some of the not-so-great ones, she thought, sipping her wine.

"Absolutely," he nodded, though he didn't smile.

A resigned confirmed bachelor, perhaps. Someone who had given up on love.

Something that she was very close to doing herself.

"Well, I suppose we should sit," Doug said, as the tables around them began to fill.

Gabby picked up her place card and set it back again. "And why exactly did you want to sit next to me versus anyone else?" She lifted her chin, trying to read the other name cards at the table. A few women who must be out-of-town guests, Doug's brother, of course. No other men, it would seem, except... Her shoulders dropped as an older man took the seat across the table and grinned at them before reaching for the breadbasket.

Much too old for her.

She dropped into her chair, and Doug was silent as a few reasonably attractive women joined them at the table, darting eyes in Doug's direction. From somewhere behind Gabby, she heard the clearing of a throat, and there, at the table nearest them, was Carol Monroe.

Gabby jutted her chin at Doug. "I think your mother's trying to get your attention."

Beside her, she heard Doug groan, and with a heavy sigh, he leaned back in his chair, turning his head. Because Gabby was now curious, she glanced over at the other table, where Carol was now making less than subtle expressions at the women at table twelve. She heard Doug curse under his breath as he righted himself in his seat, reaching for the breadbasket, his jaw tight.

One last look at Carol revealed a disappointed sigh before she pushed back her chair and hurried over to them.

"Gabby," she gushed. "I just wanted to thank you so much for putting together that exquisite arrangement. I think it was your best work yet." She gave her son a less than subtle look. "Don't you agree, Doug?"

After a beat, he nodded. "It was very pretty."

"And so are you tonight, Gabby!" Carol wasted no time in taking that bait, and Gabby had to bite her lip to keep from laughing as Doug visibly squirmed in the chair beside her. "Look at you two. Why, it seems like just yesterday you were going head to head on the debate team. And now you're all grown up."

"Not much has changed though," Gabby said with a little smile. She slid her gaze to Doug who was yanking at his tie.

Carol, however, was undeterred. She gave Gabby a little pat on the shoulder and said, "Guess we'll see about that." She widened her eyes on Doug before she scooted back to her table.

"Oh, I see what's going on," Gabby said with a laugh. "Your mother is trying to play matchmaker."

"That obvious, huh?" Doug gave her a little grin. It was a nice grin, Gabby thought. Not that she would let that sway her opinion of the man. He was still arrogant, opinionated. Infuriating.

"And you'd rather talk to me than any of these lovely single ladies?" She took another sip of her wine. She knew better than to feel flattered.

"I'd rather sit between two people that won't pepper me with small talk all night," Doug said.

Justin had joined them by now. He looked even more out of place than Doug, if such a thing were possible. The woman to his other side was trying to chat him up, and Justin pulled at his tie nervously.

Gabby looked over her shoulder to see if Carol had noticed this, but fortunately, she was laughing at something her husband said, no longer interested in what was playing out at table twelve.

Curious, Gabby turned back to Doug. For once, she was going to watch him squirm. "So, you're telling me that even if the perfect woman for you was sitting right here at this table tonight, you would rather sit quietly eating your dinner than get to know her?"

He looked at her for a long moment, his eyes steady on hers, giving her a chance to take in his full lips and square jaw.

It tensed before he spoke. "There's no such thing as a perfect match."

She should have known, but old habits died hard, as the saying went. "Maybe you just haven't met her yet."

He shook his head. "You mean to tell me that in a world as big as ours, there is one perfect person out there for each of us?"

Gabby had once believed this. She still wanted to, even if she was beginning to lose hope. But now, sitting here as the band played in the distance, and the crystal clinked, and the flowers were in full, fragrant bloom, and the bride was so radiantly happy, she dared to believe it all over again.

"I'd like to think so," she said.

He was still staring at her, and now he raised an eyebrow as a little smirk curved one corner of his mouth. "What if my perfect match is living in a small village in…Russia? What if I never have a chance to go to Russia? How would I ever find her?"

Gabby narrowed her eyes. He really was incorrigible. Still, he was tapping into her worst fears, too. She hadn't met her perfect match in all her years of Blue Harbor. There was no guarantee that she ever would.

Her gaze drifted to the bride and groom, who were now posing for the photographer near the cake, an exquisite three-tiered confection in white and lavender.

"Well, I for one think that they make a very cute couple." The bride had summered here growing up and could think of no better place to have her wedding. Gabby couldn't agree more.

"Cute fades," she heard Doug say.

Her eyes widened. Was he seriously doing this? Now? At a wedding?

"What are you? The angel of doom?"

His smile was wry. "Divorce attorney."

She fluttered her lids. Well. There it was. A man who saw more marriages end than begin. A man who was cynical and jaded. A man who didn't believe in romance. Or, it would seem, love.

She ate her dinner in silence, telling herself that Doug was probably happy for the lack of small talk, maybe even as much as she was. Really, the last thing she needed was to spend another minute in his company, being baited by his endless counterpoints, questioning everything she had dared to believe in.

"Well, I should go," she said with a sigh once she'd finished the main course.

Doug looked alarmed for a second, and if she didn't know better, perhaps disappointed. "You're not staying for cake?"

"Sorry, plans." With her bath salts and her romance novel, even if he had started to sour her taste for romance.

She swept her eyes around the tent, to the dance floor that had already started to gather a small crowd as the music picked up, and felt a longing that was far too close to loneliness pull at her heart. She loved to dance, but the only dance partners she could ever rely on were her sisters.

"Enjoy your plans," Doug said, and she felt her smile slip, because much as she was looking forward to soaking her feet in a hot bathtub and escaping into the pages of her novel, she had a very bad feeling that for her, the only place romance existed was in fiction.

4

Gabby's favorite spot in town—though she could never reveal this to her cousin Amelia who owned the Firefly Café—was Buttercream Bakery, the newest food option in Blue Harbor and sole contributor to her tightening waistband. She wasn't complaining, though. The double chocolate brownies were worth every extra lap around the duck pond, and it wasn't like she had a hot date to worry about. Or any date at all.

"You're sighing," her cousin Maddie observed, as she plated a thick and chewy brownie and passed it over the counter. "Let me guess? Your love life?"

"Easy for you to say." Gabby handed over the cash, knowing she would put the change in the tip jar. All the Conway girls supported each other this way. They'd grown up working at their family orchard and winery and they'd slowly discovered the joy of owning their businesses. It had just taken Maddie a little longer to find her confidence and go out on her own, but when she did, she'd made a whopping success of it. And found love in the process, with her contractor.

She thought back on her conversation with Doug at the wedding Saturday night, infuriating as it had been. In a world this big, was there any guarantee in finding the person who was meant for you? It was just so easy for some people.

Gabby sighed, then flushed. "Guilty as charged."

"You know what I'll say…" Maddie just raised an eyebrow.

Gabby shook her head. She knew what Maddie would say. It was what Brooke said. And Amelia. And Jenna. And her cousin Britt. And, well, everyone. She was too picky.

"I don't see what's wrong with holding out for the right guy," she said.

"Maybe the right guy is right in front of you, and you aren't even aware of it because you're too busy checking your boxes and deciding that he's coming up short on a few things."

"I don't have a checklist!"

Maddie couldn't fight off a smile.

"Well, maybe a mental one," Gabby finally admitted. "But what's wrong with having some criteria?"

"A lot of things, judging by the way it's working out for you," Maddie said pertly. She turned to take a tray of fresh cookies from her assistant and began adding them to a basket with a pair of tongs. "Face it, Gabby, not all men are like the heroes in your books."

"No," Gabby agreed, thinking of Doug again. Clearly, they were not. "But it's nice to think they could be."

Maddie just shook her head and moved on to the next person in line. It was crowded today, but then, it was always busy, especially now during tourist season. Gabby scanned the tables, happy to find a spot in the corner where she could enjoy her brownie and her book before she went back to the shop and began working on the florals for the next bride's happily ever after, because contrary to what her family members were telling her, other people were finding soulmates, and her order forms were proof of that.

She slid into the chair and pulled out her book, breaking off pieces of the fudgy brownie as her eyes scanned the page, quickly pulling her into a world so much different than her own, where a man named—

She paused, startled by the sense that someone was watching her, and looked up to see none other than Doug Monroe looking down at her. There was a definite sheen to his eyes, one she had frankly seen too many times and hadn't missed in the slightest.

"Good book?" Yep. His mouth twitched.

She closed it firmly and lifted her chin. "Excellent."

"So I see." His gaze glimmered. "I didn't mean to startle you. You looked so immersed."

She pinched her lips harder. "I was, and if you don't mind, I think I'll get back to it."

"Actually, I was hoping you might be willing to share your table," he said, looking only slightly apologetic.

Gabby glanced around the room, disappointed to see that every table was completely occupied, including the ones set up on the outside deck, and that she was, technically, hogging the last free chair in the bakery with her handbag.

"Oh." She felt flustered as she set down her book. "Um, sure."

Doug wasted no time in dropping into the seat as she hooked her handbag over the back of her chair. She blinked rapidly at her brownie, wishing she hadn't bought it, or at least had the sense to get it in a white paper bag. Instead, it sat on the pretty painted plate, virtually untouched, meaning that unless she crammed it into her mouth and drew further potential cause for judgment from the man who was now unloading files onto her table, she was stuck sitting here for at least ten minutes. Yes, ten minutes until she could politely make up an excuse and be on her way. So much for a relaxing break in the day.

She stifled a sigh and wearily picked up her book again, miffed to see that she had forgotten to mark the page in her haste.

"Here you go," Maddie said, coming to the table with a steaming mug that was again, much to Gabby's disappointment, ceramic and not paper. And now Doug was settling in nicely, hooking an ankle over the opposite knee, smiling up at Maddie as if she had just delivered him a winning lottery ticket rather than a simple cup of coffee.

So he respected some people's career paths, just not hers. Not that she couldn't say the same about his life choices. Divorce attorney. Pfft.

She must have scowled because she caught Maddie giving her a strange look through her smile.

Oh, no. No. Maddie was getting notions, and Gabby was having none of it. Doug had been bad enough back in high school, and by the looks of things, not much had changed. Well, other than his looks, of course, but that was far from her priority. After all, as many had been quick to point out, Jackson Bradford had high marks in the looks department, but that didn't make him an eligible romantic suitor. Deep-set eyes and a strangely alluring albeit infuriating grin couldn't qualify Doug Monroe for that category either.

But Maddie didn't seem to know or care about any of this. And now she was chatting happily with Doug, welcoming him back to town, saying how pleased she was that he was here to stay, giving only slightly subtle glances to Gabby as she did so.

Gabby rolled her eyes when her cousin finally went back to the counter.

"I think she's hoping more will come of us sharing a table than just coffee and a brownie," Doug said, breaking the tension.

Gabby couldn't help but smile. At least it was out there, rather than simmering between them.

"Welcome back to Blue Harbor," she said, somewhat sarcastically. "But yeah, everyone in my family is always trying to set me up, especially before my uncle's wedding at the end of next month."

"Singles table again?" His brow lifted.

She hated to admit it, but there was little sense in stating otherwise. "I'll be with my sisters. Well, one sister. Brooke is married. Well, back together with her husband, I mean."

Oh, it was a long and convoluted story, and though the gossip had flown through town all spring faster than the birds returning from the southern states, Gabby now wished she hadn't said anything.

"They almost got a divorce?"

Was a six-year estrangement almost a divorce? Gabby wasn't the judge of that. She broke off a piece of brownie and stuffed it in her mouth. Nine minutes more. Then she would leave.

"Disappointed you didn't get the business?" she asked, thinking of the very few people in town who had split up over the years. There were Maddie's boyfriend's parents, years ago, and a few others, but not enough to keep food in the fridge for a divorce attorney, unless Doug decided to market to other towns.

She frowned at that, wondering just how it worked. "And how is business?"

"Oh, I'm just getting settled." Doug took a sip of his coffee, leaning back in his chair, but she sensed a faint pull between his brows. Trouble, no doubt. "But I'm always happy for referrals, so if you hear of anything…"

She laughed out loud. "In my shop?"

"Well, you said that people send flowers for all sorts of reasons. I just thought, if there were any sympathy requests…"

Now Gabby nailed him with a look. A hard one. One that said he was ridiculous and had crossed a line. He lifted his palms. "Joking, joking."

Only she wasn't so sure that he was.

She picked up her book again, rifling through the pages until she found the scene that she'd just finished, where the hero decides to book a trans-Atlantic flight to get back to his beloved before she marries the wrong man.

Yes, there was nothing worse than ending up with the wrong man. A wrong man was worse than no man at all. And if she had to sit at a singles table for the foreseeable future while she waited for the right man, then so be it.

Only right now, she wasn't single at her table. She was sharing it. And Doug was once again turning out to be a difficult tablemate.

The table shook as he dropped a thick file on it, nearly spilling his coffee. She met his eye across the table, hoping he sensed her irritation, but he just stared right back, forcing her to notice the way his eyes crinkled slightly at the corners, making him seem almost…friendly.

"Do you mind?" he finally asked, breaking the silence, and it was only then she noticed that he was waiting for her to move her brownie so that he could consume the entire table—her table—with his paperwork.

"Not at all," she said, wondering if he'd picked up on her tone. "I need to grab a napkin anyway."

She dropped her book onto her chair as loudly as she could, which unfortunately wasn't very effective considering its size, and strode to the counter, knowing that if she didn't get a break from this man, she might do something really stupid…stupid like throw out her brownie or give it to him, just so she could leave. And right now, that brownie was turning out to be the only good thing in her day.

"Everything okay?" Maddie asked, looking far too amused for Gabby's liking.

Gabby paused, considered asking for a paper bag for her brownie, and then decided against it. It would be letting him win, wouldn't it? It was what he wanted. For her to give up her table, let him have it all to himself. Well, no. Two could play at this game.

"Oh, other than the fact that Doug Monroe has decided to put his paperwork all over my table?"

Maddie stifled a laugh. "Well, technically that's *my* table, and I thought it was sweet of you to let him share it. He could have just taken his coffee to go. Instead, he chose to sit with you."

Gabby frowned at that. Nothing about this situation implied that there had been a choice in it.

"Did you miss the part where I said he was crowding the table with his stuff?"

Maddie lifted her chin and took stock of the situation across the room. "Looks like a nearly even split to me. And remember our conversation just last week? The one where we talked about compromise? Do you think I like having to watch half of Cole's shows each Friday night?"

Gabby hadn't considered something as simple as this.

"I don't enjoy it any more than he likes all the cooking contests I watch," Maddie said with a shrug. "But I do like the company, and that's what it's really all about, right? Otherwise… Well, if you want life completely on your terms, then you're better off alone."

Better off alone? Gabby couldn't even believe her cousin would say such a thing, and to her of all people, who decorated weddings and devoured all things romance more than Saint Valentine himself.

She plucked two napkins from the stack and said nothing more as she went back to the table.

"I brought you a napkin," she said, sliding it over his stack of contracts. She didn't want to see the names on the files, didn't need to see whose dreams had shattered.

"How thoughtful!" His grin was coy.

"I consider myself a thoughtful person," she said matter-of-factly. "It's why I'm so well suited for my job. Sometimes it's the little details that make the most difference."

"I couldn't agree with you more," Doug said.

She looked at him in surprise. "Really?"

He nodded firmly. "It's the little details that are the most overlooked, in my experience. Most couples are so busy focusing on the big picture that they aren't noticing the small things that will end up becoming big deals in the end, like she didn't know that he was a teeth grinder, or he didn't know that she always has to shower before breakfast."

"That sounds very petty," Gabby said flatly, and then, thinking back to her recent conversations with her cousin felt herself twitch. She pursed her mouth and sat up straighter. "I hardly believe that people end their marriages over…nuisances."

"Not directly, but it all has to reach a tipping point at some point. There's a reason why the percentage of couples who can't make it 'til death do they part is so high."

"I like to think that there's someone out there for everyone," she said, refusing to be pulled down by his cynicism.

"So you said." His look again told her that he wasn't buying into it.

"Obviously for every couple that doesn't make it, another does." She clung to the thought of her family members, who had weathered the tough times, laughed through the good ones. "You just have to be sure that you're marrying the right person."

"And is that why you're still single?" he countered.

She sniffed, refusing to take it personally. "I am holding out for the right person, yes."

He raised an eyebrow but said nothing as he took a sip of his coffee. The silence that stretched between them made her grind back on her teeth.

"I get the impression that you think otherwise?"

He set his coffee mug down on the table. "I just think that most people believe they are marrying Mr. or Mrs. Right on their wedding day, when in fact, they are very sorely wrong."

He waved some papers in the air and he let that soak in, which she had to admit, she couldn't find a rebuttal for, but she would in time, oh, she most definitely would.

"And this is where I come into play. Prenuptial agreement. Every single person should have one before they say those two magic words. *I do*." He grinned, and she felt her eyes narrow.

"Tell me, what is it that has you so against the idea of everlasting love?"

"Easy," he said with a shrug. "It's a fantasy." He tapped on her book cover, which she pulled back defensively, holding it to her chest. So it might have a prince on the cover. The heroine was a commoner! "People like the fairy tale. Make an entire business out of it. The gown. The shoes. The shows. The books." He picked up his mug again and paused. "The flowers."

Well, that did it. "And does this theory of yours come from personal experience or just your professional experience?"

"Both," he said, surprising her.

She blinked at him, wondering what he even meant by that, and then deciding that it didn't matter. The man was an anti-hero, no grand gestures here, no sweeping overtures, certainly no simple, thoughtful acts as small and sweet as giving a flower. And she wasn't going to waste another minute of her precious time on him.

The world was full of men, better looking than him, too. Those deep-set eyes? Eh. Okay, yes, appealing, but really, overrated. Yes, quite overrated, along with that devilish grin he was now giving her.

She realized with a newfound fury that he was enjoying this!

Composing herself as best she could, she calmly placed—well, shoved—her book into her bag, set her napkin over her brownie, and wrapped it up quickly. "I just realized that I have an appointment, so the table is all yours."

"Shame," he said. "I was starting to enjoy the company."

She set the wrapped brownie on top of her book and looped the handles of her bag over her shoulder. "The company or the banter?"

"Was that what it was? Either way, it was like old times."

There was that phrase again.

"Yes, well, old times are often better left in the past." She stood, eager to leave, but found herself off-kilter, not knowing exactly what to say before she finally departed from the table once and for all.

Across the room she saw Maddie watching her over the table, giving her one of those wide-eyed stares that made it clear she was growing quickly exasperated by Gabby's refusal to just fall in love and marry whichever random Joe came along or commented on the weather!

No, this little debate had confirmed it. There were the right guys and there were the wrong guys, and Maddie happened to have just found a good one on her first try.

"I'd tell you to have a nice day, but given the direction of our conversation, I assume you'll just tell me that it's going to be terrible, so why bother trying to enjoy it." She sighed down at him, and after a moment of silence, he erupted into laughter. Long and loud enough for several other patrons to stop their conversations or look up from their books and turn and stare.

Gabby caught Maddie's eye and shook her head as she clutched her handbag and headed to the door, the sounds of Doug's laughter still roaring in her ears.

Yep, she thought, just like old times. And just like their high school days, she wasn't about to back down easily. Doug Monroe had met his match!

5

Saturdays meant weddings, and this one was just as lovely as the last, Gabby thought. If not more so, because it was set right on the sandy beachfront, evoking a perfectly summery, casual vibe that made Gabby want to kick off her shoes and wiggle her toes—if she didn't have work to do.

The bride had asked for simple bouquets, and Gabby was always happy to accept that challenge. Sure, it was easy to get swept away and let the flowers be not only the center of the tables, but the center of attention as well, with grand arrangements in large scales, or covering every square inch of surface. She'd seen plenty of this in the magazines she subscribed to each month, and she'd also followed through on several bride's wishes for just such thing. But there was so much to be said for letting the natural beauty of the flowers' colors and textures speak for themselves.

Now, as Gabby took her seat at the singles table, sighing deeply after a long day on her feet, she was quite pleased to see that the mixed arrangement felt fresh and light and added a boost of color to the otherwise all-white décor.

She swept her eyes over the rest of the tables, smiling at the way everything had come together, from the warm day to the soft lake breeze, to the quintessential feeling of summer in Blue Harbor, but her smile immediately slipped when she saw Doug Monroe standing near the bar that had been set up near the band, a glass of red wine in one hand, looking about as lost as she currently felt.

What was Doug doing here? Her mind swam as she considered her options, her eyes darting to the place cards on either side of her, happy to see that the names were of men she'd never heard of before, probably cousins or friends from out of town. Single men. Eligible men. She sat up a little straighter and smoothed a palm over her low ponytail, wondering if she could discreetly add some gloss to her lips without anyone noticing.

Too late. She watched in growing dismay as Doug's eyebrows shot up and, with dread, he began walking in her direction.

"We meet again," he said, dropping into the seat beside her. "Let me guess. All these flowers were your doing?"

She pursed her lips. "My creation, yes."

"You must go to a lot of weddings," he observed.

"I do," she said, nodding. "And I suppose you go to a lot of hearings."

"When business is booming," he said, taking a sip of wine.

"You mean when people's lives are unraveling?" She tsked. "It doesn't tire you to benefit from the misfortune of others?"

"I consider myself to be a helping hand. Someone to support them and their interests when they need it the most." His mouth tipped into a grin. "You could say we help each other out. You help people get married. And I help them get…unmarried."

The hood of her eyes drooped. "I think I need a glass of wine," she said, standing. Only hers would be white wine because red wine at weddings made her twitch. Already she spotted a stain on the tablecloth at the next table over. "And just so you know, there's no sense in trying to claim that seat as your own or switching the name cards. I know who is supposed to be seated to my left and my right."

"You know them then?" He shuffled some cards around. Gabby noted that he was now seated beside his brother.

She couldn't completely fight off her hopeful smile. "Not yet. But...I'm looking forward to knowing them."

He nodded sagely. "Of course. I suppose if you believe in love and happy endings and all that stuff, then you are also optimistic enough to think that every single eligible person you meet could be the one."

"Not every single person," she said pointedly. "But yes, I do believe in all that...*stuff*."

With that, she turned and made her way to the bar, cursing under her breath as she did so, wishing that at least one of her sisters or friends from school had been invited, but the bride and groom were a fair bit younger, and the bride was relatively unknown to anyone but her, seeing as the groom had been the one to grow up in town.

And down the street from the Monroe family, she thought, rolling her eyes skyward. She should have known better.

Sure enough, Carol waved to her eagerly from across the crowd. The poor woman; she had pinned her sights on the wrong woman, and Gabby hated the thought of letting her down. She took her time at the bar, sipping her crisp white wine and waiting for the crowd to thin and most guests to take their seats before she made her way back to the table, hope swelling in her chest when she saw her empty chair and the backs of two male heads on either side, one fair, one medium brown.

Doug caught her eye from across the table as she approached, seeming to hide a smile she couldn't quite make sense of, until she slowly pulled out her chair, and found herself sitting next to a teenage boy.

Well, maybe he was more like twelve.

"Hi!" He grinned to reveal a mouth of metal braces, complete with food wedged in a few brackets.

She swallowed hard. Managed a nod. "Hello."

She licked her bottom lip, refusing to make eye contact with Doug, and oh so subtly glanced to her right, her heart skipping a beat when she caught the handsome profile of a man of the appropriate age. Nut-brown hair, strong jaw, and a lovely, warm smile when he turned to introduce himself.

"Guess we're stuck with each other for the night," he said, and oh, those dark eyes positively twinkled as he extended a hand. "Jeremy Smith."

She felt herself melt into the warmth of his skin. "Gabrielle Conway."

She could have sworn she heard a snort from across the table, but she decided to ignore it. She had better things to focus on just now.

"And what do you do, Gabrielle?"

Oh, her name just rolled off his lips. Smooth and deep, she could get used to a voice like that.

"I own a flower shop here in town," she said, feeling her spirits rise as they did every time she mentioned her business. "Sweet Stems?"

"Oh, now, don't be humble, Gabby!" Doug's voice seemed to boom across the table.

She narrowed her eyes at him, even though the smile never left her lips. Was he really going to taunt her, now, when she finally had an eligible man giving her a little attention? Last she checked, they weren't in high school anymore, even if he was determined to act as if they were.

Ignoring her glare, he said to Jeremy. "Gabby did all the flowers for this wedding."

Jeremy raised an eyebrow. "Really? This is very impressive. I've always marveled at anyone with a creative mind. It's a talent I'm afraid I've never had."

She resisted the urge to slant a glance at Doug, but she did lift her chin a notch. "Thank you," she said warmly. "And what do you do?"

"Pediatric oncology," he said flatly.

She managed not to gasp. Handsome, noble, and smart? Every box on that mental checklist was being ticked. This was turning out to be the perfect night—that was if Doug wasn't continuing to watch their exchange as if he had a front-row seat to the latest Hollywood blockbuster.

The waiters came around with their first course—a summer salad made with locally grown tomatoes and herbs—but Gabby had more important things on her mind than food.

She had never seen this man before, and this was a wedding. She couldn't rule out the possibility that he lived far away, nixing her hopes. With a silent prayer, she decided to confront the only obstacle that might eliminate the chances of this being the man of her dreams. Her soulmate. Her perfect match.

"I haven't seen you around Blue Harbor before," she said conversationally. When he met her eyes with a slow grin, she somehow managed not to bat her eyelashes. "Are you in town just for the wedding?"

Here it came. She almost couldn't breathe, so great was her anticipation.

"The hospital is about two hours from here, but we have a weekend place in Pine Falls."

Pine Falls was the next town over, but this didn't bring any relief to Gabby. *We*? What exactly did he mean by that? With her last thread of hope, she wondered if he was referring to his parents—a family vacation home perhaps, but she knew she was grasping. She scanned his face, wondering what she had missed.

"I'm afraid my wife is on bed rest so she couldn't make it tonight."

Now there was a coughing sound from across the table, followed by wheezing. No doubt Doug was trying to smother his laughter.

"I was telling the table here before you arrived." Jeremy smiled until his eyes crinkled. "We just found out we're having twins."

Twins. Somehow, she managed a thin smile and a grunt of congratulations before reaching for her wineglass and taking a long sip. Over the rim, she caught Doug's grin flashing wickedly and narrowed her gaze. She could nearly hear a "told ya so" coming on. No doubt he'd find a way to slip it into a conversation before the night was through.

With a heavy heart, Gabby picked up her outermost fork and listlessly poked at her salad, hating the tears that had started to burn the back of her eyes and hoping that they would clear before she was forced to look up again. She positioned herself in her chair so she was slightly facing the boy instead, but he just gave her a hopeful look and then went all red in the face. Good grief. She sensed a shuffling beside her, a murmured conversation. Maybe the handsome doctor needed to take a call. She'd do almost anything for him to be gone when she looked up.

Finally, when she'd composed herself, she dared to check, startled to see that her wish had come true. Technically. Gone was Mr. Right and in his place was…Mr. Wrong.

"What are you doing here?" She glanced at Doug and then to his former place across the table, where the hot yet married man was already engaged in a conversation with the bride's younger cousin about name ideas for his twins. Two boys. Imagine that.

"Saving you," Doug said simply.

More like coming to gloat! She pinched her mouth together from saying that very thing, reminding herself that she was technically still the florist, the bride was a client, and she would be best to keep her temper under control.

Doug just sniffed as if nothing was amiss, averting eye contact as he placed a crusty sourdough roll on his plate and proffered the basket to her with an extremely wide grin that seemed close to eruption. "Bread?"

Her eyes blazed when she thought of the audacity, the nerve, the presumption! Thinking that she needed saving! "I...I..." She couldn't even think, so great was her anger at the merriment in his eyes, at the way this entire evening was turning out. She'd dared to hope. Dared to believe. And now she was left sharing another Saturday night with Doug, who knew exactly which buttons to push to tap into her innermost insecurities. "Oh, fine."

She grabbed a roll from the basket and then, because carbs were so comforting, another.

She didn't have to ask before Doug slid her the butter dish, and she furiously added pad after pad to her roll, because what did it matter if she put on a pound or two or ten? No men loved her, and all the good ones were taken.

And for the second weekend in a row, she was sitting next to her nemesis, because no matter what she did, she just couldn't seem to be able to shake him.

*

Doug watched as Gabby polished off one sourdough roll, then another, and then, after checking the breadbasket and noticing it was nearly empty, he caught her eye.

"Go on," he encouraged.

"Thanks," she muttered, helping herself to the last of it.

He considered himself to be an astute observer of human behavior, though perhaps he had overestimated his skill set. Considering that he was just as thrown by Lisa cutting off their engagement as he was baffled by Gabby's funk right now, he might still have a lot of learning to do.

Curious, he finished his first course and waited until the main course had been served before turning to Gabby. "I don't think frowns are good luck at a wedding."

It was meant to be banter, but she didn't even bother to argue. He took a sip of his wine, realizing that something must seriously be wrong.

"Is this because of that guy?" he asked in a low enough voice that he knew they couldn't be overheard. The conversation was lively, and voices were rising as drinks were flowing.

"This guy, that guy, all guys." Gabby narrowed her eyes as she tore into the last roll with her teeth. She chewed angrily and then picked up her fork, making short work of the potatoes.

He watched in amusement as she ate her way through the plate, finishing it clean before he was barely halfway done with his fish.

"Well, I think you're giving this guy far too much credit, if you ask me," he said, glancing at her sidelong. When she didn't argue he pointed out, "I mean, yeah, so he's tall and has dark hair and money and saves kids' lives. If you're into that kind of thing."

Now he got a smile out of her, wan though it may be, and he grinned in return, happy to see a glimmer of the old Gabby returning and realizing that he had missed the spark in her that seemed to have gone away, however briefly.

"Sometimes it wears on me," she said. "Going to these weddings, helping to plan the flowers, making every other woman's day special. Is it too much to ask for a special day like that for me?"

"Oh, all my clients once had their day," Doug replied. "Remember that. They're probably more miserable than you are right now; in fact, for most of them, I'm sure of it. Besides, I'd like to think that it's better to be alone than with the wrong person."

Her eyes rounded as she stared at him, half a bread roll still lodged in her cheek, puffing it out in the most strangely attractive way. The Gabby he knew back in school never had a hair out of place. She was perfect, unreachable, and unflappable.

Or was she?

Gabby finished chewing and chased it down with a long sip of wine. "That's exactly what I tell everyone. I'm not just going to settle for the heck of it."

Ah, now they were getting somewhere. He nodded, because he agreed and because he was curious to sit back for once and let her do all the talking. There was no debate here, no argument to contend with, just two single people, sitting together, at yet another wedding.

"I mean, take my cousin for example. Maddie." Gabby gave him a knowing look, and he was surprised that she would even refer back to their afternoon at the bakery. She'd left in such a huff that he assumed it would be the last she'd speak to him.

Until he poked her, that was.

"She agrees with Brooke. And all the rest of them." She sat back while their plates were cleared and eyed the raucous across the tent. "Oh, good, the cake is being cut. I'm starving."

He raised an eyebrow. He was quite full himself.

"And what do Maddie and Brooke say?" he wanted to know.

"Oh." She waved a dismissive hand through the air. "A lot of things. Basically, that I'll never find everything I'm looking for."

"And what is that you want? Husband? Kids? White fence? Maybe a dog?"

"Doesn't everyone?" she sighed. She caught herself and gave him a sharp look. "Oh, that's right. Not everyone. Not you."

He opened his mouth to disagree, because that's what he did, especially when it kept her attention, but tonight he could not disagree with her words.

The problem was, he couldn't agree with them either. Sitting here, beside Gabby, at a wedding, where his parents were two tables over, holding hands, his mother laughing at something his father whispered in her ear, made him realize that he did want everything that Gabby had just listed.

He just didn't believe that he could have it.

His gaze drifted to the bride and groom now posing in front of their four-tiered cake, and he listened as their nearest and dearest gave them a heartfelt toast. He clapped along, not allowing himself to wonder what his brother or parents might have said at his wedding. He'd never really gotten that far, and maybe that was a problem.

He frowned as he sipped his wine, watching Gabby devour the icing on the cake that was set before her.

"So, you really want all this? A big, white wedding?"

"Doesn't everyone?" She paused and shook her head. "Never mind. I forgot who I was talking to. I know, you're probably going to say that this is all just a fantasy, an overly expensive party with flowers that will just be dead tomorrow. That marriage isn't about the dress and the cake. Or, of course, the flowers."

"For what it's worth, the flowers are really pretty," Doug said. He regretted what he'd said in the shop, especially when he saw his mother's reaction to the bouquet. "But you have to admit there is some truth in the fact that flowers do not last forever."

"Nothing lasts forever," Gabby countered.

His eyebrows shot up. "Says the hopeless romantic!"

She dropped her chin and gave him a pointed look. "You know what I mean. Besides, I'm beginning to feel more hopeless than romantic. Congratulations, you win."

He stared at her for a moment, hating the hurt that he saw in her eyes. He'd seen it once before, back at their senior prom, when the committee had finished a long day of setting up for the event. Gabby had lingered in the doorway, taking in the transformed gym, a strange sort of sadness taking over her features even though he had thought she was pretty happy with the way it had all turned out.

It wasn't until he asked if he'd see her later, and she said no, that he understood the root of her sadness. And as he sat home alone, looking through his college course selection book, thinking ahead to his big future, he'd wished that he'd had the nerve to let his guard down for once and ask her to join him.

He wondered now what she would have said if he had. Probably no. Or laughed. Or assumed he was just having a go with her.

Gabby finished her slice of cake and recovered the last of her icing from the plate.

"Here," he said, sliding his piece over to Gabby. "I can tell you want it more than me."

Her lips turned into a little smile. "Why, Doug Monroe, that was downright chivalrous of you."

"Don't be getting notions that I'm like one of those characters in those romance novels you were reading at the bakery," he warned, unable to fight off a smile as she accepted it and happily slid her fork through the white, sugary icing.

She laughed. "Oh, believe me, I'm smarter than that, and you have made your feelings about love and romance crystal clear." She glanced at him, her eyes taking on their light again, her smile full and kind. "But…thank you. For the cake. And…for tonight."

He grinned, finding it hard to pull his eyes away from her, but there was his mother, making excited expressions in his directions and it was probably best to excuse himself now before he gave his family any more reason to talk about his personal life or give himself any more reason to question it. He stood, slowly, and gathered his wineglass, giving Gabby one last smile.

"My pleasure. *Gabrielle*," he was sure to add because when it came to Gabby Conway, he never could resist.

6

The highlight of Gabby's month was always her cousin's book club meeting. Isabella Clark, more often known as Bella, owned and operated the only bookstore in town, and in addition to hosting poetry readings, writing groups, and story hours for children, Bella's Books was the gathering place for thought-provoking literary discussion. Or at least that's what all the ladies who belonged liked to claim.

In truth, it was a social event and one that Gabby desperately needed this weekend as a distraction from all this wedding talk. Romance, she could never tire of, but weddings... Between the endless arrangements, set up, and then attendance, she was already looking forward to wedding season being over.

"But it only just began!" Brooke laughed when Gabby confessed as much on their walk down Main Street. It was Sunday night, and the sidewalks were quiet. While Bella typically held the monthly meeting on Saturday nights, during tourist season (and wedding season!) it had become easier for everyone to attend at the end of the weekend instead.

Gabby closed her shop on Sundays, usually spending the morning at the family's market at the orchard where she sold bouquets that people liked to buy for their dinner table, followed by lunch at the Carriage House Inn, or lately, to support her sister's husband Kyle at Harrison's Pub, a dive bar which was starting to undergo a recent renovation since his brother Ryan had moved back to town. Ryan, she knew, was single, and easy on the eye, too, but he fell under the category of family in her opinion, and with his focus on his business above all else at the moment, he was definitely not marriage material.

And that's what she wanted, she thought. Marriage. Or at the very least, love.

"It's all the late nights," Gabby explained away her complaints, knowing she should be grateful for the business.

"You know what I'm going to tell you…" Brooke raised her eyebrows. "If you would hire a proper assistant rather than ask Mom to pitch in—"

"Mom likes helping out!" But Gabby knew her sister had a point. She'd been too tired and too busy to stop by the town event last weekend, and with the way things were going, she'd probably miss the orchard's annual Cherry Festival, too. She didn't know how she was going to set up Candy's wedding and be a proper guest, too, not that she'd be letting those doubts be voiced. She'd get it done; she always did. And in the end, she was always satisfied with the results. She wasn't so sure the same could be said if she tossed another person's ideas into the mix.

"Besides, it's not just the prep and set up. Not every bride, but many, were sweet enough to extend an invitation to stay for the reception, and I don't feel like I'm in a position to turn them down."

"But you don't have to stay long, just make an appearance." Brooke paused as they approached the storefront, where a black urn of overflowing Annabelle hydrangea sat beside the paned glass door. "Unless you have a reason to stay?"

Gabby rolled her eyes. "Please. I'm stuck at the singles table every time." Her mood deflated when she recalled her disappointment last night. A tall, dark, and handsome doctor. She'd thought she found the one, and instead she'd made a fool of herself, starting to flirt with a man who had already announced he was married to the rest of the table! And an expectant father to boot!

"As you said, singles tables usually contain single men."

"If by men you count teenage boys or men whose pregnant spouses are on bed rest and couldn't attend, then sure."

Brooke laughed and clamped a hand over her mouth when she saw that Gabby didn't find any of this to be amusing. "No."

"Oh, yes." Gabby shook her head. "The only single men at my table last night were the Monroe brothers."

Brooke frowned as she pulled at the large brass handle and they both stepped inside the bookstore. The smell of the paper always comforted Gabby, as did the possibility of perusing the new release table. There was always an escape to be found between the pages of a novel. And a guaranteed happy ending, too.

"Brothers? Is Doug back in town?"

"Moved back a few weeks ago." Before her sister could get any notions, Gabby added, "Hasn't changed one bit."

She realized that wasn't exactly true. He had of course filled out in all the right places, and there was a rumble to his laugh that hadn't been there fifteen years ago. Still, he was argumentative and opinionated. But he did let her have his cake. And that was…nice.

Gabby lifted a paperback from the table of new releases and turned it over to skim the back copy.

"Still sparring with you then?" Brooke gave a little smile. "You know, it's funny, but I always used to think he just did that to get your attention."

Gabby looked at her quizzically as she set the book down. "Well, he's a grown man now who doesn't need to tease to talk to a girl. And he's still up to the same old tricks." Her mouth thinned when she thought of the more glaring fact that would immediately shut down this conversation. "Also, he's a divorce attorney."

Brooke just shrugged.

"And I'm in the business of romance," Gabby reminded her. "We both are."

"Oh, yes you are!" Candy, who had clearly caught the end of their conversation, wiggled both sets of fingers as she eagerly crossed the room.

Oh, brother. Gabby had forgotten that the book club's switch to Sunday nights made it easier for Candy to attend, since the Firefly Café was closed on Sunday nights and Mondays.

She caught her sister's eye quickly, wondering which of them would be targeted first. With Candy's wedding now only three weeks away, there was very little time for major changes. Or any changes at all, really.

"Now, Brooke, I've been thinking more and more about that train…"

Brooke shook her head. Her time in New York had made her more assertive than she'd been as a kid, but it was her reunion with her husband that had really lifted her confidence. She was doing what she loved—designing her own creations, running her own business, and coming home every night to a home she shared with the love of her life.

Brooke made it all look so easy, Gabby thought on a sigh. Still, she knew that it had been a rocky path, but one that had been worth it in the end. She comforted herself with those words as Candy continued to fret.

"Don't think, Candy. Just…enjoy this special time." Brooke even managed to smile while she said this, but Gabby knew she'd be heading for the tray of wine soon. "Everything will be perfect. And you did truly want that twenty-five-foot train."

Candy was chewing on a fingernail. "I did. And I even thought at one point that it might not be quite long enough…"

Gabby scurried away before Brooke heard her snicker, or worse, Candy turned her attention to the flowers which were absolutely not changing. Nope, if she had to make up a story about inventory or flooded crops that damaged some new-fangled idea, so be it. She had listened, patiently, and she also knew that Candy would be thrilled with the result.

As usual, Bella had set up chairs in the back of the room, near the children's corner, and tables had been cleared of books and replaced with drinks and snacks.

Gabby set her contribution on the table—a bottle of white wine—and went ahead and helped herself to a plate of cheese and crackers.

"Uh-oh." It was Bella, smiling at her. "You only hit the buffet like this when you're upset. And usually, it's about a guy." Her eyes went wide. "Is there a guy to be upset over?"

Like her, Isabella was single, only it didn't seem to bother her quite as much. Gabby dropped her shoulders and shook her head as she added more cheddar squares to her plate, and, for good measure, some nice creamy gouda.

"No. There is most certainly not a guy to be upset over." She frowned slightly, realizing that had Bella posed the exact question to her this time yesterday, she might have named Doug as the source of her problems.

But last night Doug hadn't just been a perfect gentleman; he'd been a friend of sorts, or at least an ally.

Pushing that thought away, she went back to her cheese. "And how is your love life these days?"

It was refreshing to turn the tables on a cousin who was just as single as she was these days. And always, Gabby corrected herself. It wasn't like she'd gone through a breakup, hit a dry spell, or had a teen romance to fall back on—she didn't even have a first love. A first crush, sure, but nothing ever came of it. She'd dated a bit, mostly seasonal tourists, or the occasional guy from Pine Falls, but there had never been a spark, and she had only been disappointed that she didn't feel anything toward the man, rather than be upset that nothing more came of it.

"Hey, I thought we were here to talk about books." Bella was always an expert at shifting the topic without getting herself worked up or offended. "Did you enjoy this month's selection?"

This month's selection had been a classic—Austen—and who could go wrong with that?

"I think you know the answer to that," she replied with a laugh, already feeling her spirits lift being here in her second favorite shop of all of Blue Harbor, next to her own—not that she'd be telling Brooke that—with a cousin who loved books with romantic endings every bit as much as she did, and Candy, still busy trying to convince Brooke to hack five feet off the train she would no doubt want ten feet longer the week before her wedding.

Bella caught her smile. "There's the cousin I know. By the way, I meant to tell you, that guy who always used to give you grief back in high school was in here the other day."

"Doug?" Gabby nodded and popped another bite of cheese and cracker into her mouth. "Yes, he moved back to town."

"So he told me. Here I thought when I saw you so upset…"

"That I was upset about him?" Gabby covered her mouth to laugh. "The only thing to get upset about when it comes to Doug Monroe is how mad he always makes me! He loves nothing more than a good argument."

Bella gave her a funny look. "I just thought…because back in high school, you used to talk about him just as much as that lacrosse captain—"

"Soccer captain," Gabby corrected, thinking of Chad, who would strut down the hall with that cocky grin, his hair always tousled, his eyes so blue. She nearly set a hand to her stomach to stop the swoon, even though she hadn't seen him since the summer after graduation. Like many people in Blue Harbor, he'd gone away to college and stayed away. But Gabby could never bring herself to leave this lakeside town that had always been her home. Even if she was starting to wonder what the future could hold for her here.

"You know what I mean." Bella poured herself a glass of white wine. She was a Clark, a relation on Gabby's mother's side of the family, and even though she was in no way related to the Conway orchard, she was always happy to support the business by proudly displaying their local wine at her club meetings.

"No," Gabby said, honestly. "I don't."

Bella leaned in, giving her a sly smile. "Doug got to you."

"He *annoyed* me," Gabby corrected.

Bella gave a little mew. "Isn't it one and the same? Besides, he's pretty cute. I don't remember him being that cute."

"He wasn't," Gabby said, before catching the spark in her cousin's eye and realizing she had inadvertently agreed with her. "Look, there's nothing between Doug and me, not then, not now."

"You're sure about that?" Bella asked.

Gabby didn't pause to consider it. "I know the kind of guy I'm waiting for, and I can promise you, he is most certainly not it." She thought of the way he made sure to goad her into an argument every time she saw him, the way he seemed hell-bent on showing just how much he disagreed with her career choice, her opinion, her optimism. The man was rude, really. And he was far too cynical for her liking.

Bella just nodded and took a sip from her glass, saying nothing.

"If you're going to try to tell me that opposites attract—" Gabby started to say, but she was interrupted by Bella's hoot of laughter.

"Oh, honey. You don't need to worry about that. You and Doug were never opposites. You were more like…two of a kind."

"Did I hear someone say two of a kind?" Candy was back, and Gabby and Bella exchanged a brief but knowing glance.

Candy helped herself to a giant cookie and looked at Gabby with interest. "We aren't, by chance, talking about a certain bartender in town?"

Gabby suppressed a sigh. Candy wasn't going to let this Jackson thing drop. For so many reasons, Gabby's life would be easier once Candy had sailed off on her honeymoon, she reminded herself. After much discussion, the couple had decided on a two-week cruise, and Gabby suspected it would be the most relaxing fourteen days that any of the Conway girls would experience for the foreseeable future.

"Bella and I were just talking about an old friend from school," Gabby said, not mentioning that it was a male

friend and that she and Doug had never really been friends at all.

That according to Bella, they'd been two of a kind.

Looking disappointed, Candy took another cookie and went to her favorite seat, the chair beside Bella, even though the meeting hadn't yet started, and no one would dare take Candy's seat, knowing that if they tried, she'd bat her eyelashes and plead with them to trade.

Two of a kind. As if! Gabby was still frowning into her plate considering her cousin's words, when Bella touched her on the shoulder, made her excuses, and tapped on her heels across the room to where her sister Heidi was standing with Helena, the town librarian.

Normally, Gabby might have joined them, but she was too unnerved by what Bella had just said. Besides, she hadn't even mentioned to her cousin that Doug was insistent that he didn't believe in love—not for himself. Maybe not for anyone.

Gabby set her plate down on the table and noticed a stack of new romances on the table beside it, most specifically, the latest in one of her favorite series, guaranteed to have a swoon-worthy hero and the happiest of endings.

Maybe she should take her sister's advice. Take a break from looking for love for a while. At least she could always find it between the pages of a book.

*

Doug pulled his frozen dinner from the microwave and peeled away the plastic cover, knowing that his mother would insist he join them for Sunday night dinner if she had any idea what he was eating. It was another reason that he didn't want to share too many details of his personal life. His parents knew about the breakup, of course, and the last thing he needed was his mother worrying too much, because her type of worry usually led to problem-solving, and that, he feared, would lead to matchmaking.

Make that more matchmaking. She'd called twice to not so casually mention that he seemed to be having a nice time at the last two weddings. The less he said, the more she pressed. It would seem that she had made it her mission to see her eldest son settled into a relationship. One that preferably led to marriage.

He'd tried to tell her that he was happier this way, but she was his mother, and she tapped into the small part of him that wasn't so sure that this was true. And damn it if she wasn't determined to make it all better, the way she'd always done, even when he was younger. Only now the wounds couldn't be bandaged or forgotten about with an ice-cream cone. Now the only way to ensure he never felt that sort of pain again was to stay clear of it.

The game was on the television, a hot plate of lasagna ready to be enjoyed, and a six-pack of cold beers on the bottom shelf of the fridge. Sure, they were the only thing in the fridge, but he hardly had time to grocery shop between work and all these weddings.

A knock on the door interrupted him as he was grabbing a plastic fork from the stash he kept from the delivery bags he'd collected since his return.

"It's open!" he called, knowing that it would be his brother, who lived one floor up in this old mill at the edge of downtown that had been converted into apartments years ago.

"Smells good in here," Justin remarked, sniffing the air.

Doug laughed. "If Mom could hear you, she'd be dropping off casseroles for a month."

"Would that be so bad?" Justin opened the freezer, which, opposite of the fridge, was packed with frozen entrees, and then closed it, opting for a beer instead. "I was going to see if you wanted to grab a drink in town." He cracked the top of his can, taking a long sip.

"Another night," Doug promised. He'd gotten used to staying in and relaxing with the television for company, but having his brother nearby was a good change of pace. He pulled over two unpacked boxes that were currently being used as a makeshift coffee table and motioned to the couch. "Make yourself at home."

"I'm not staying long. Some of the guys are at Harrison's, watching the game together."

Doug nodded. Since coming back to town, he hadn't gotten out much, not that he had anything against the guys he'd once called friends in school. Or at least, acquaintances. Truth was he kept to himself back then even more than Justin did. But whereas Justin's excuse was that he was quiet and reserved, Doug's excuse was that he saw high school as a steppingstone for college and then law school, not as an experience to enjoy in the moment.

Tonight, he was drained. Tired from two weekends in a row of socializing, fielding probing questions from nosy former neighbors who wanted to know if he met anyone special yet. Tired from spending his days establishing his new practice, dealing with the stress of the calls he took from the few clients he'd taken on. It was enough to turn the most romantic guy into a realist, not that he'd ever been romantic.

Or so Lisa had said when she'd ended things.

"You thinking of Lisa?" Justin pointed to the spot between his eyebrows. "You get this little pinch there every time her name gets mentioned."

Doug raised his hand to his forehead. Caught. "Nothing to think about. We dated. I proposed. She called it off."

"You seemed pretty caught up in conversation with Gabby Conway last night," Justin said, smirking.

Now Doug scowled as he popped the top on his can of beer. "And you're starting to sound like Mom." A thought stopped him mid-sip. "Tell me she's not going to try to pair us up."

"Are you kidding? She pulled me aside when the dancing started to ask me what I'd overheard at the table."

"Here I thought she was trying to push me onto some of the other single women at the table."

"Oh, I think that was just her way of feeling out how much you preferred Gabby." Justin's grin was broad and gloating. He was enjoying this entirely too much.

"Gabby and I are just old friends," Doug said, and then paused, realizing that he wasn't so sure this was true.

Sure enough, Justin said, "Since when? You two were at each other's necks back in school."

"Only because we were always after the same things," Doug said. They hadn't been friends, but they hadn't been enemies either. If anything, it was because of Gabby that he'd felt compelled to push himself harder, strive further, be the best that he could be.

"It was more of a healthy competition we had going," Doug summarized. Yes, that was all it was.

"She's still pretty," Justin said, and as there was no arguing with that, Doug could only nod. With her long auburn hair and sharp green eyes, there was no trying to deny the fact that Gabby was a beauty.

"Yep, always was." His mouth thinned. Enough talk about Gabby Conway, or his love life, and definitely not in the same breath. "You sure you don't want to stay?"

Justin set down his beer and shook his head. "You sure you don't want to come?"

If heading out with his brother meant more questions about the state of his personal life, he'd rather sit out. Besides, Kyle Harrison was married to Gabby's sister Brooke, and even though he had handed the bar off to his brother recently, he still probably frequented it on nights like this.

"Early morning tomorrow. Prenuptial papers. Usually a draining experience, sometimes ugly."

"Next time then." Justin backed up to the door and pointed at him. "And I won't take no for an answer."

The door closed with a click and Doug turned the lock. The apartment felt suddenly very quiet, too quiet, and he picked up the remote and cranked the volume on the television, but it didn't help.

His brother was good company, but the truth was that the only person that Doug enjoyed chatting with these days was Gabby Conway. He'd always liked chatting with her—or arguing, if one might call it that. It fired him up, got his blood pumping, excited him in a way that he hadn't felt in a long time. Not since high school, really.

He shook his head, slid his fork through his lasagna, and took a big bite.

He'd gotten used to spending time with a woman these past few days. And that was probably something he shouldn't turn into a habit.

He'd just need to get out more. Be amongst the land of the living. Remind himself that he wasn't completely alone. But that he was most certainly better off not sharing his life.

7

On Thursday evening, Gabby closed up her shop and let herself into the door beside it, before hurrying up the long flight of stairs to her apartment on the top floor above Sweet Stems. She had spent too much time helping a kind, older gentleman pick out flowers for his wife for their anniversary, and now she had about ten minutes to change and get ready before making it to the Carriage House Inn in time to meet her sisters for a midweek dinner.

Jenna usually ran late with her piano lessons, and Brooke could be held up by a client. Gabby hoped to snag the best table before things filled up, as they were known to do, especially during the summer months when tourism was at an all-time high, even during the weekdays.

Her apartment was small, but cozy, with creamy white walls and pops of color in her throw pillows on her blue sofa and all-white bed. She rummaged through her closet, wishing that Brooke still lived in the little apartment over her shop so that she could borrow something—but Brooke was back to living with her husband, of course, and now Jenna had recently taken the apartment instead. After nearly six years in New York and a fashion career under her belt, Brooke could always be counted on to look stunning wherever she went, and even better, she was always happy to share her closet. Other than close proximity, the same could not be said for Jenna, who was happy in casual attire or overly formalwear reserved for her concerts or other performances.

Gabby exchanged the cotton sundress she'd worn all day for cropped jeans, a white cotton top, and her favorite gold metallic sandals. With a quick comb of her hair and a touch of lip gloss, she was back down the stairs again, tapping out a text to her sisters just as one appeared on the screen.

It was Brooke. Stuck at work. Running ten minutes late. Oh, and did she know that Jenna couldn't make it? A make-up piano lesson for a student who had been sick last week.

No, Gabby had not known this, and she was disappointed that her youngest sister would be absent, but still, she was happy to use the time to discuss Candy and some other clients that she shared with Brooke. Gabby had the impression that this kind of talk made Jenna feel left out, even though she was sometimes asked to play piano at a wedding ceremony.

Gabby took the side entrance to the pub, bypassing the front lobby entrance of the Carriage House Inn, and was dismayed to see that it was already filling up. She considered sending another text to her sister, suggesting they meet at the Yacht Club instead, but there would be no way they'd get a table on such a gorgeous summer night at the waterfront restaurant, especially not at this time of evening. Firefly Café would be equally busy with their lakeside deck, but Amelia had been known to "find" a table for her in the past.

Gabby considered this for a moment until she remembered that Candy now worked at the café nearly full time.

She kept her eye on the dining room of the pub as she made her way to the bar, just as a couple was sliding off their stools. Perfect! She hopped onto one, tossed her bag on the other, and grinned with satisfaction. Until she saw the man sitting next to her.

None other than Doug Monroe. And from the amused look on his face, he'd witnessed the entire thing.

"I didn't realize you would be so eager to see me!" His eyes seemed to twinkle.

She gaped at him. "I…I…I just…" She could feel the heat flare in her cheeks as she struggled to find a diplomatic response.

Fortunately, he started to laugh. "I'm joking. Obviously, this is a surprise for us both."

A pleasant one? She had to admit that she didn't exactly feel as fired up as she normally did when she caught that smirk. Besides, he had helped her out last weekend, and she still hadn't properly thanked him for it, either.

"I'm waiting for my sister Brooke, but she's running late," she explained. She eyed his beer, which was almost finished. "I owe you a drink anyway."

He cocked an eyebrow. "I would have thought by your notion of romance that the man should do the buying."

She swallowed hard, laughing nervously. "Well, this isn't a date, and there's nothing romantic between us. I just wanted to say thank you, for last weekend."

He didn't argue with her but just gave a little knowing smile. "I don't share my cake with just anyone, you know."

She felt her cheeks flush again, only this time at his words, not hers.

Jackson was behind the bar, and he came over, a look of obvious interest passing through his eyes when he glanced from her to Doug and back again.

The look she gave him in return was withering.

"A white wine for me and another beer for Doug. And I'll start a tab. Brooke and I are having dinner."

She didn't need to look at the menu to know what she'd be ordering—a juicy burger with a side of truffle fries. She'd been coming here since she was a kid, and the cook had stayed all these years. It was something she'd come to count on, she supposed. A reason why she stayed. Blue Harbor may not have offered her the exact life she'd been hoping for just yet, but what it did offer, she knew she couldn't replicate anywhere else.

She glanced at Doug, wondering if the pull of this small community had been the reason for his return.

"Kyle joining you guys?" Jackson asked as he poured the drinks and handed them across the bar.

Gabby shook her head. Kyle was still in the process of transitioning management of Harrison's to his brother, Ryan. It would take time, and he'd still be invested, but he now had the opportunity to pursue his true passion, making hand-carved furniture that looked more beautiful than anything she'd ever seen in a store. It was a reminder to her that things worth waiting for came in due time, and that she could try to be a little more patient and enjoy the journey.

"Ladies' night tonight." Her grin was only mildly apologetic.

Jackson and Doug exchanged a look and Doug held up a hand, grinning, "I was here first."

"And there were no free tables," Gabby was quick to add.

Jackson just shook his head. "I think you both protest too much." With a low rumble of laughter, he flung a towel over his shoulder and walked to the opposite end of the bar.

Gabby stared after him and then slanted a glance at Doug. "Ridiculous. Don't mind him. Everyone in this town is just determined to set me up."

"Join the club," Doug snorted.

"I take it your mother hasn't backed off?" Gabby couldn't help but like the camaraderie. Her mother was quiet with her opinions, but Candy was far from shy, and Maddie wasn't far behind.

"Ever since I moved back." Doug shook his head. "They don't think I'll be happy until I meet the right woman. Can't seem to understand that I'm perfectly fine, just as I am."

Gabby went quiet at that. Here was a man who was determined to stay single, not that it should matter much to her. Except that the more time she spent in his company, the more she was starting to think that there might be more in common between them than she'd first thought.

"I have another wedding this weekend. Client gig. But my mother has still taken it upon herself to inquire about the seating arrangements and guest list. She happens to know the manager of the Yacht Club. Popular place for weddings, it would seem."

"The McBride wedding?" Gabby was suddenly alert. She'd been reviewing the order form today, checking her inventory, calling the flower market to be sure that her orders would all arrive in time.

His gaze snapped to hers. "Don't tell me—"

She laughed. "I'm doing the flowers."

"You're really in demand, aren't you?"

She felt her smile slip as she stiffened and sipped her drink. "It's a full-time career, and admittedly this is my busy season."

He cocked his head to the side, giving her a little nudge. "I see that now. You've turned me into a believer."

Her eyes sprung open. "Is that so? You're actually admitting that I'm right?"

"I'm admitting that I see your point about the benefit and allure of flowers, yes."

"And here I thought I had turned you into a believer about love."

His eyes went flat and for a moment she wondered if she had touched a nerve. But he just took a sip of his beer and said, "Can't see anyone convincing me of that."

"I suppose if all these weddings can't change your mind, then it's a pointless argument." She sighed. "Although, I'm starting to get a little tired of filling all of my Saturdays this way."

"You're not alone. Looks like we'll be stuck with each other for another Saturday night. Could be worse, right?"

He gave her a long look, one that made her finally look away.

"It beats a root canal," she said, sliding him a rueful look.

"Or a blind date," he said, raising an eyebrow.

Leave it to him to have a better retort. Like always. "Okay, you win. But thankfully, I haven't ever been subjected to a blind date." Though at this rate, Candy was probably sure to find a way to make that happen. What Candy didn't seem to understand was that she didn't want to force love. She wanted to find it.

"I was thinking," Doug said slowly, "that if we're both stuck at another singles tables, we might think about going together. Or at least being each other's wingman. You know, in case you're seated next to another preteen."

"Beats the married man," Gabby said with a laugh. And for the first time all week, she suddenly found it all very funny, rather than so disappointing.

Doug covered his mouth, trying to hide his growing smile. "You should have seen the look on your face when he mentioned his pregnant wife."

"You should have told me!" she scolded. But she knew that there was no way he could have, and she should have seen the gleam in his eye as fair warning that something was brewing.

With a nod of her head, she decided that setting herself up for more letdown was worse than spending another evening next to Doug. It would take the pressure off the situation, allow her to just enjoy herself rather than walk into every event hoping that this would be the night she'd find the one. Brooke would be pleased when she told her—if she wasn't going to read way too far into it first.

She held out a hand to Doug. "Okay, you have a deal. We'll be each other's wingman. If your mom tries to set you up with someone you're not interested in, you can say that you're keeping me company. Perfect excuse."

"At least you know the conversation will be stimulating." He slid her a grin as his warm hand took hers, and something deep inside her flip-flopped at the size of it, the way his skin was pressed against hers, and the way he held it firmly, but gently.

Quickly, she snatched her hand back, making his smile a little wider. It was a nice grin, almost devilish, and she liked the way his eyes crinkled at the corners. It was the same grin he'd always given, but back in the day, she'd found it annoying, even menacing. Nothing could fire her up more. Only now that fire felt...

Her heart was racing as she reached for her wine, happy that it was chilled the way she liked it, and hopefully capable of taking her body temperature down a few notches.

In her periphery, she spotted her sister, and turned to see her weaving her way through the pub, a look of surprise on her face when she saw whom Gabby was sitting with.

"Doug Monroe," Brooke said pleasantly. "How nice to see you again." She glanced at Gabby and said, "I'm happy to find you two in one piece. She hasn't been too hard on you, has she?"

"Quite the opposite," Doug said pleasantly. His gaze traveled to Gabby and lingered there. "I think Gabby and

I have discovered that we're better off joining forces than pushing each other away."

Now Brooke's eyebrows shot up dramatically, but Doug's gaze never left Gabby's as he slid off his stool. "I'm off, ladies. Enjoy your night. And I'll see you Saturday, Gabby."

Gabby couldn't even speak as she pulled in a breath, knowing that Brooke had to pinch her lips together from saying anything, and waited until Jackson had slid a glass of wine to her without having to be prompted. In typical fashion, Brooke took a slow sip of the drink, leading Gabby to think she might be off the hook long enough for her to think back on the strange turn of events, and to remember that grin, and the way it made her stomach roll over.

Brooke opened the menu, casually skimmed the first page, and then darted a glance over her shoulder.

"He's gone. Now tell me exactly what is happening Saturday night."

Gabby laughed. "Nothing. We're both attending the same wedding."

"From what I heard, I thought maybe you were going together."

Gabby considered her words, thinking of the truth in them. "More like...hanging out together. It beats talking to strangers at the singles table."

"But the singles table is where the eligible men are," Brooke reminded her.

Gabby wrinkled her nose. "I think I'm finished pinning hopes that the guy I'm supposed to end up with will be someone I meet at my singles table. Besides, at least with

Doug, there's no chance of anything happening between us, so there's no pressure."

Brooke didn't look convinced. "What is it then?"

"Just…someone to talk to," Gabby said with a shrug. "There's absolutely nothing more to it than that."

Brooke didn't look convinced as she went back to her menu. "If you say so. But if you ask me, you two look really cute together."

"I thought *we* looked really cute together," Jackson said, leaning over the bar and giving her a wink.

She swatted him away, and he happily took their menus after taking down their orders. Gabby sighed after him, thinking of Candy's determination to see them set up. Adorable, yes. Trouble, yes. Exciting, yes. But he wasn't looking to settle down.

And neither, she reminded herself, was Doug Monroe.

*

Doug stopped by his office instead of heading home. The empty apartment full of boxes was nearly as depressing as the small practice that wasn't seeing enough business. He hadn't expected things to grow quickly, but he also couldn't shake his conversation with Gabby at the bakery last week either—not any more than he could shake the one they'd had tonight.

Gabby was right, about a lot of things, not that he'd be telling her so. No, it was much more fun to watch her pretty little mouth pinch and her eyes blaze. To have her full attention. It was thrilling, now as much as it had been years ago, but that's where it stopped. Hanging out with

Gabby was fun. It was stimulating. It made him feel alive again.

And contrary to what she believed, he didn't mind being proved wrong. Only right now, when he looked at his schedule for the next day and saw that he had no appointments, he minded a lot.

Weddings were taking place every week. Divorces, not so much. The town was small, the population too, and the neighboring towns weren't much bigger. Still, there might be some truth in the fact that people were happy here. That this community pulled people together rather than drove them apart.

His parents were shining examples, after all. Even during the tough times, their spirit hadn't been tampered any more than their mutual affection. His mother still laughed at his father's bad jokes, and his father still looked forward to the same casseroles that Doug's mother had been making since before he was born.

If he was being honest with himself, he couldn't remember Lisa laughing at any of his jokes, at least not in their last few months together. But then, they weren't that kind of couple. Sure, they made time for trips and dinners, but their conversation revolved around their careers. As two attorneys, there was always a story to share, an idea to bounce, and their drive to succeed was mutual.

But if he was going to have any success now with his law practice, he had to put a lot into consideration. He wasn't working toward partner anymore; it wasn't about taking on the biggest clients or billing the most hours. He was here to serve the community, but he wasn't so sure that they required his services, and that was a bittersweet thought.

He'd never been good at compromising—Lisa had pointed that out during their arguments over the wedding plans. They both forged ahead, both locked into ideas, both thinking of the endgame instead of the big picture and somehow losing sight of their relationship along the way.

The past year had been derailing, stressful, and uncomfortable. For as long as he could remember he'd made a plan and stuck to it, spoke up for what he believed in, argued his points without backing down. Lately, nothing had gone as planned, despite his efforts, and change had become inevitable, even when it wasn't on his terms.

Feeling tired, he straightened up some paperwork and tucked a copy of his latest contracts into a file folder, sitting at his desk to open the bottom drawer.

His hands paused on the knob when he saw the framed photo that had once sat on his desk in the law firm, the one of him and Lisa at their official engagement photo shoot—one of many boxes they had checked as part of their plan to have a perfect wedding.

He shut the drawer abruptly and turned on his laptop before his mind could wander again. Work had always been his driving purpose, just like grades had once been. It was something he was good at, something that came easily to him and made him feel like he was on a path, even if it wasn't always the one he'd wanted to follow. He'd never been one of the popular kids, never all that athletic, at least not when it came to team sports. Back then it had bothered him, but eventually, he'd thought it had paid off. He'd gone to his first-choice college, then law school, and then started up with a reputable firm, eventually making junior partner.

But when Lisa called things off, he felt directionless for the first time in his entire life.

Even now, after coming back to his hometown, he still felt a little lost and unsure. Of his future. His business. And his heart.

8

The McBride wedding was one of the bigger events that Gabby had on her list for the summer—both the bride and groom came from money, and she supposed she wasn't completely surprised that Doug had handled their prenuptial agreement, even if it did contradict her romantic notions. Ever popular, the reception was again held at the Yacht Club. Gabby watched the ferry boats come and go as she finished setting out the centerpieces. Rather than a tent, the couple had opted to use the on-site pavilion, and the bright pink roses set on the crisp white tablecloths looked beautiful against the lush green grass and white painted building.

The weather had held up too—blue skies that would result in a clear night that would guarantee stars twinkling above.

The water lapped at the rocky shoreline as Gabby adjusted some votive candles, even though they wouldn't be lit until dusk, and by the waitstaff. Her duties were officially over, and from a distance, she could hear the cheer of the crowd from the other side of the docks where the couple had decided to hold an open-air ceremony. No doubt, the bride and groom had just been pronounced husband and wife.

Gabby sighed to herself and then made the round to the singles table, where she saw that her name card was already positioned between Doug and— She blinked, not quite sure she was reading it correctly. But it was right there, in pristine, black calligraphy. Chad. Her old crush. Soccer captain, teen heartthrob, barely seen in Blue Harbor since he'd gotten that athletic scholarship to a college out east after graduation.

And evidently, he was still single.

Her heart began to race as the guests began their walk over from the docks, coming around the side of the building that divided the two spaces. She scanned the people, looking for a hint of dark hair, baby blue eyes, a grin that made her weak in the knees, and a swagger that could make any girl swoon.

No one fit the description.

Disappointed, she wondered if he hadn't shown at the last minute. It was known to happen, and it would be just her luck too. Determined not to let her hopes get too high, she walked across the grass to the open bar and happily accepted a glass of chilled white wine.

She needed to keep a clear head if she was seeing Chad again after all this time, but she was also so nervous her heart was pounding, and her eyes kept darting over the gathering crowd, finally resting on Doug.

He gave a little smile and crossed to her. "Looking for me?"

"Actually, I saw at the table that Chad Johnson is here. Do you remember him from school?"

As if anyone could forget him! Not only was he the most popular guy back in high school, but he was also the most attractive. He was prom king both junior and senior year, which he attended with Nina Payne, head of cheerleading, of course. Gabby had solaced herself with this cliché when he hadn't asked her both years in a row, even considered trying out for the squad, but it wasn't her thing.

Doug, however, didn't look impressed. "Ugh. Always a bit of a jerk, wasn't he?"

Gabby stared at him, taken aback. "That's not the impression I had of him."

"Impressions have no facts to back them up. They're rather loose opinions, if you ask me." He was having fun with her, she knew, but she was too nervous to bother with banter at the moment.

She gave a little smirk. "Good thing I didn't."

He narrowed his eyes on her for a moment, as if there were something he wanted to counter that with, but seemed to let it drop when he accepted a glass of wine from the bartender.

"Who else is at the table?"

"I didn't look much beyond that. And I'm afraid I didn't recognize the woman on the other side of you, so there's no telling what you're in for," she added.

Doug's brows shot up. "Thanks for the warning."

Gabby grinned, feeling a little more relaxed, but she was still scanning the crowd, feeling further disappointed when no one fitting Chad's description jumped out.

Eventually, they made their way to the table, which was already filled up with a few women she knew from town, and a few she didn't. A portly man was sitting in the chair beside hers, and she was just about to kindly ask that he find his assigned seat when he looked up and she realized with a shock that she was looking at Chad. Those eyes were unmistakable even if the rest of him was…different.

"Gabby Conway?" He grinned that same grin that was certainly resistible now and motioned for her to sit down. "Thought that was you."

Had she changed that much? She laughed nervously. No, she had not. Her hair was still the same, her style too, whereas Chad… So he had doubled in size, she told herself. It wasn't just his good looks that had caught her attention all those years back. It was his laugh, his good nature, his achingly charming demeanor. He had charisma, something not many boys back then had. Certainly not Doug.

She swallowed hard and pulled back her chair, noticing the surprise flit through Doug's eye as he did the same. It would seem that it had taken him a moment to recognize Chad, too.

She heard the low rumble of laughter beside her as Doug took his seat. She kept her chin high, inhaled and exhaled. Slowly.

"And Doug Monroe!" Chad said loudly. "Remember the nickname we used to have for you?"

Gabby saw Doug's mouth set. "Oh, Chad, after all these years, I'm sure you have better things to do with your time than think about high school." Though his tone was good-natured, there was a decided edge to it.

"I can see you haven't changed at all!" Chad laughed heartily, as if expecting everyone else to get the joke, but seemed unphased when they didn't and politely went back to their own conversations.

Gabby looked at Doug, but he refused to meet his eye. His jaw tensed when he reached for his glass.

Chad slurped his wine and set it on the table with enough force to cause some of the red liquid to slosh onto the formerly crisp, white tablecloth. Gabby felt her blood pressure rise. The reception had only just begun and already this table was stained. This was how wedding gowns were ruined. It was a good thing Brooke wasn't here to witness this; Gabby was fully aware that Brooke had to resist asking everyone who entered her shop to wear gloves.

She darted a glance to the head table, hoping that the bride stayed away and that Chad was the only inebriated guest, especially this early into the reception.

Chad casually flagged the waiter over and accepted a fresh glass of wine from the tray, and then he extended his other hand, grabbing a second glass.

For a moment, she thought it was a chivalrous gesture—even though she would never run the risk of drinking red wine at a wedding—until she watched in horror as Chad triumphantly set both glasses in front of him.

He winked at her. "Best part of a wedding, if you ask me. Free booze."

Gabby felt her back teeth graze.

"So, Chad, what have you been up to? You went to Penn, right?" She told herself that it wasn't sad she remembered this fact. Blue Harbor was small and details like this were shared, even if years had passed since Chad had been back to town.

She saw Doug's eyebrow twitch when she reached for her wineglass. So yes, she'd remembered this detail. She'd remembered a lot about Chad. Sadly, she could probably still recite his senior year schedule if she tried, because of how many days she'd orchestrated passing by his locker at the exact right time.

"For a year," Chad said. "Got injured at the end of my first season. Didn't have the grades to keep my scholarship either, so, I was out."

She blinked at him, then tried to take extreme interest in her salad course. "Oh, did you transfer?"

"No, just started doing odd jobs here and there. Eventually got married. Had a kid." He wiggled his left hand. "Divorced now."

She gave him a look of sympathy. "I see. I'm sorry." She waited for the hope to build in her chest the way it might have once, but nothing was there.

His eyes narrowed, and his gaze drifted somewhere into the distance. "Better off. She was bad news, but not as bad as my second wife."

Gabby felt her eyes widen as she reached for the bread-basket, which Doug all too eagerly passed to her without having to be asked. It was going to be another comfort food night. No sense in worrying about getting lettuce stuck between her teeth either.

Through the remainder of the salad course, she listened to the details of Chad's first marriage, from the brief run-ins with the law for unpaid parking tickets and other "misunderstandings," as he was sure to tell her, to the child he never saw, to the support payments he was still expected to send.

By the time the main course had been set before her, Chad had moved on to the details of his second marriage…and his next set of wine, because she didn't know what else to call it. A pair?

She sipped her drink miserably and looked over at Doug, who was supposed to be her wingman, after all, only to realize that he was seated beside a woman who wouldn't stop adjusting her hair and batting her eyelashes, giggling nervously.

While pretty enough, it was clear that she was eager and didn't have very much to say, and that Doug was having about as miserable a time as Gabby was.

He caught her eye, seeming to exhale in visible relief.

"Excuse me," he said politely to the woman beside him as he started to stand, "but I've ignored my date all evening and I promised her a dance."

The woman looked so disappointed that for a moment, Gabby felt bad as she pushed back her chair, until Doug grabbed her elbow and whispered in her ear, "She has hamsters. Three of them. And I now know more about taking care of hamsters than I ever wanted to."

Gabby hooted in laughter.

"I suppose you owe me for saving you tonight, then." She was all too happy to even the playing field, but as Doug led her to the dance floor, he had a gleam in his eye.

"You're not off the hook yet. Besides, you didn't seem to be having any fun with Chad. Didn't you have some big crush on him back in high school?"

Her cheeks flamed, even though that was nearly half a lifetime ago. "How did you know?" Surely just knowing where he'd gone to college couldn't have given her away.

"It was pretty obvious at the time," he said, then, seeing her horror, laughed. "It was a long time ago; does it really matter?"

"Does any part of high school matter?" She shrugged, not sure of the answer to that, and sensing the way his smile drooped, she wondered if Doug felt the same. "Well, do you think we're free of them?"

Doug looked over at the table. Sure enough, the woman who had been chatting with him all evening wiggled her fingers and gave a little smile. Doug groaned and looked away.

"She likes you," Gabby teased. It was nice to be on the other end of their banter for once. "And you never know, you might love hamsters if you give them a chance."

"I suppose we should probably dance," he said to that.

Gabby sucked in a breath, suddenly feeling a little nervous. She had assumed it was just an excuse for an easy escape, a chance to break away, maybe hit the bar instead. One dance, and then she could probably leave.

She wished a faster song were playing, but knew that part of the evening was still a ways off, and that by then she'd be home in her cotton pajamas, tucked into bed, with a good book for company. Suddenly, that thought no longer seemed so comfortable, or appealing. And it certainly wasn't a good way to find what she was looking for in life.

The problem was, she wasn't so sure what she was looking for anymore. And as Doug turned to face her, and casually slipped his hand around her waist while reaching down with the other to take her hand, she felt herself stiffen, as if every nerve in her body had gone on high alert.

"This feels like prom all over again," she muttered, trying to ease her discomfort at their proximity. His hand was warm in hers, the other tight on her waist, and he moved with ease.

"I thought you didn't go to prom?"

She looked up at him, surprised that he would remember that, much less know it. She'd been so involved in the prom committee that most people hadn't noticed that she hadn't stayed for the dance. But Doug had noticed. He noticed a lot about her, she was starting to realize, swallowing hard as she took in his deep-set eyes that showed no hint of amusement or menace.

"I didn't have a date," she said simply, breaking his gaze. It was a sore spot, even now, that she'd put so much thought into the planning of the event never to enjoy it. Really, it was ridiculous that she still felt a tug in her chest over something that had come and gone more than fifteen years ago.

"You could have had any date in that school. Most guys were just intimidated by you."

She felt her cheeks flushed, but she shook her head. "I'm over it. You don't need to flatter me to cheer me up."

"Oh, it wasn't a compliment."

She pulled back slightly, giving him a hard look, and he quickly added, "I just mean that you were one of the prettiest girls in our grade. In the school really. But you were selective, and you had high standards, and I think a lot of guys were afraid to take that on."

In other words, she was picky. Gabby's head swam as she considered his words, along with the endless advice she received from her sisters and cousins. Did he mean what he said? That she was one of the prettiest girls in school?

She chanced a glance at him, feeling suddenly shy and a little off balance. She took a step, but it was the wrong one, and instead of her heel hitting the floor, it landed squarely on his foot.

"Sorry," she said, even though she was almost grateful to cut the tension. "I've never been much of a dancer." Never had much experience with it, even though she enjoyed it. More than she probably should at the moment. "Another reason to scare off the men, I suppose."

"I could draw up a disclaimer for you. Steps on feet while dancing." He grinned, and she felt a strange sort of flutter in her chest.

"You were never afraid to take me on, though," she pointed out. "You had no problems speaking your mind around me, and not just on the debate team. I'm still mad at you for putting up such a stink over the artificial snow machine I wanted to bring in for the Winter Wonderland theme." Not, she thought, that she would have been there to enjoy it. Still, there had always been the hope that she would be asked.

"Ah, we're back to prom then." His grin was rueful.

"Why did you join those committees?" He was the only boy on the prom committee, a good male influence, others pointed out, even if he frustrated her to no end with the way he always had to counter each of her opinions with one of his own.

He paused for a moment, looking over her shoulder before shrugging. "Looked good on college applications."

She thought about it, knowing just how important his academic path was to him back then. It was the same reason he'd given back then, too.

"Well, it paid off. You went to law school. And now you have the career of your dreams."

"Oh, now, I wouldn't say it's the career of my dreams."

She faked surprise, though the truth was she couldn't believe he'd admit such a thing. Doug had always been defensive and still was from what she'd seen. But there was a softer side to him, too. One she was just starting to notice.

"Are you telling me that you don't enjoy helping people dissolve their marriages?"

"Believe it or not, I'd much rather see people live happily ever after. I just know that isn't usually the case. Eventually...well, eventually life has a way of getting the better of people."

"You sound like you're speaking from more than just professional experience," she noted, wondering if there was more to Doug's attitude about love than he was letting on.

"Take your teen heartthrob over there for example," Doug pointed out. "You thought he was the greatest guy in the world and look at him now. Imagine if everything

had gone the way you had hoped it would. He asked you to the prom, you had a magical night, you started dating, got engaged, maybe even married. He'd still be who he is."

She glanced over her shoulder at Chad, who was now making a sloppy effort of hitting on hamster girl.

"He certainly changed," she observed.

"He didn't change," Doug said. "He's just a bigger form of the jerk he was back in high school."

Chad's earlier taunt came back to her. She opened her mouth to ask Doug about it and then stopped herself. In school, Doug had been lanky, not exactly athletic, and more interested in books than sports. She hadn't considered that he might have been picked on for that. That maybe, it was part of the reason he was so firm with his opinions in places where his words were heard.

"I didn't realize Chad was that way. I guess…" She frowned, thinking back on her cousin's words. How the right guy could be in front of her all along and she wouldn't even notice it.

Same went for the wrong guy too, it turned out.

"I guess I just saw what I wanted to see," she finished.

She glanced up at Doug, her breath catching at the way he was looking at her, wondering if he realized that something about tonight didn't just make her see Chad for who he was.

It made her wonder if she'd misread Doug all this time, too.

9

Gabby was just putting the finishing touches on a birthday arrangement for a sixteenth birthday when the bells over her shop door jangled. She braced herself, knowing that Candy liked to pop in on Mondays when the café was closed, but right about now, she was almost happy to look up and see her future aunt and most high-maintenance client walk through the door. The rain had been falling all morning, meaning that aside from phone orders, activity had been slow, leaving her alone with her flowers, her work, and her overactive mind, which seemed to be on repeat mode, replaying Saturday night over and over until she'd almost forgotten she was still standing at her workbench.

So Doug had turned out to be a surprisingly good dancer; it wasn't like she had many others to compare him to. And she did like to dance. Didn't have the opportunity to do it often enough. Really, she had just gotten swept up in the moment. It was easy to do so at weddings…

She finished fluffing out the rest of the greenery and set the vase to the side for delivery. Wiping a hand across her brow, she smiled at Candy, who was smoothing down her wet hair.

"Hello, Candy! What brings you out on a day like this?" She wagered Candy's motive was an even split between wanting to change her centerpieces or discuss Gabby's love life.

"Oh, I was looking in some of the shops for bridesmaid gifts," Candy began. All four of Uncle Dennis's girls would serve the role. All, Gabby had been told by Brooke, who had been asked to design the bridesmaid dresses, would be dressed in pink.

"How nice," Gabby said, knowing that Candy's true motive was yet to be revealed. "Did you find anything special?"

"Oh, well, since they're all so happily settled into fulfilling relationships, I thought maybe something like…a wedding planning book of their own."

Gabby burst out laughing. "But none of them are even engaged!"

"Yet." Candy put a finger in the air. "And you know it's just a matter of time."

Gabby couldn't disagree with her there, even though she was rather sure that her cousins wouldn't appreciate Candy meddling further in their personal lives. But Britt had been back together with Robbie Bradford, her high school sweetheart, for about a year now, and Amelia wasn't far behind with Robbie's cousin Matt. Even though Maddie and Cora were settling into newer relationships without a previous history, it was clear that both were happy and in love.

"Yes, I do think they have each met their perfect match." She felt her smile slip a little, as the old feelings of self-pity reared. She imagined being in the same position, to have someone to talk to at the end of the day, share a meal or a glass of wine with, laugh over the good things, cry over the bad.

Lately, the only person she'd confided in was…well, Doug didn't count. He was just someone she knew well enough, and saw often enough, to have some things to bond over. There was nothing more to it than that.

Firmly, she reminded herself again of his difficult personality, his infuriating need to be right all the time, even though he had sort of softened on that stance, never mind the fact that he was a divorce attorney and a confirmed bachelor.

Her lookbook was on the counter, and now Candy leaned forward with interest.

"These are pretty…" Candy tapped a finger on a photo in the binder. Gabby prickled at the tone, knowing that Candy was all too easily influenced by new ideas, even if they weren't her true style.

"That's the wonderful thing about flowers," she told Candy kindly. "All of them are pretty."

They shared a smile, but Candy gave a wistful sigh.

Seeing the need to rein things in, Gabby said, "Those are ranunculus. They were in the first design we agreed upon and you decided to eliminate them by the third round."

"Did I?" Candy gave a slightly embarrassed laugh. "Gabby, the way you say it makes it seem like I've changed my mind over and over again."

Gabby blinked at her. Willed herself to be quiet. Told herself the client was always right. That the wedding was now less than two weeks away, and then Candy would be on her merry way, off to her honeymoon, giving all the Conway girls a chance to breathe for a little while.

"I was just tweaking things," Candy explained, giving her a dismissive wave before flicking to the next page. "Oh!"

Gabby pinched the inside of her cheeks to stop herself from bursting out laughing when she saw the photo that had caught Candy's eye. "You like that one?"

"Like it?" Candy set a hand to her heart. "I *love* it, Gabby. Oh, I don't mean to be difficult, but this photo of this arrangement… It's perfect. Truly perfect. No more tweaks needed."

"Good, because that's your arrangement," Gabby said, giving her a sly grin. She'd slipped that in there after the last sample she'd created for Candy, simply because she'd been so happy with how it looked, but now it seemed that her effort had paid off.

"It is? It looks different here than in the photo I have." Candy began rummaging through her oversized pink binder for the last contract she and Gabby had settled on. There were several pages from the shop, Gabby noticed. Candy's cheeks turned pink as she leafed past them, not admitting that there were numerous changes, and not all of them were tweaks.

But here, at last, they had indeed settled on the perfect arrangement, and hopefully Candy's mind would be put at ease once and for all.

"I took these in a different light, that's all," Gabby said. "The colors may look a bit lighter in my photo, but that is also how they will look in the chapel and at your reception." On gloomy days like today, her shop was cozier and dimmer than most wedding days turned out to be, and thankfully so.

Candy pulled the final contract from her binder and compared the two photos, giving Gabby a dramatic pout once she'd confirmed that they were, in fact, the same. Gabby straightened her workspace while she waited for Candy to get to the real reason for stopping by today.

"Will you be at the Cherry Festival this weekend?"

"I'm going to try!" It was the one free weekend in Gabby's foreseeable future, and as much as she enjoyed the Conway Orchard and Winery event each year, she didn't want to commit too soon. Besides, she could tell by the gleam in Candy's eye that she was getting at something.

"I love that orchard. It's the perfect location for my rehearsal dinner, don't you agree?"

Gabby nodded, assuming the question was rhetorical.

Finally, after shoving everything back into her bag, Candy opened her eyes with strained innocence. "Have you given any more thought to a plus one for my wedding?" she asked, and Gabby wondered if this was the point of her visit. Would redesigning her bouquet for the umpteenth time be an easier task? Possibly.

"Nothing is going on between Jackson and me," Gabby said firmly. "Never was. Never will be. He's handsome, but he's entirely too much trouble."

"And here I thought you liked that roguish charm," Candy said mischievously. Their shared love of romance novels was common knowledge.

Gabby shook her head. "At this point in my life, I'm not looking to change anyone. Years ago, sure, that would be exciting, but Jackson is a flirt, and…I'm looking for forever."

"Nothing wrong with a woman who knows her mind!" Candy nodded her approval.

Gabby moved some cuttings into the trash can and wiped down her workstation. "Try telling that to my sisters. They seem to think that I'm getting in my own way of finding true love."

"They think you're holding out," Candy nodded, as if this too, were common knowledge.

Gabby realized with a start that it probably was, at least amongst her own family.

"They think I'm too picky," Gabby said.

"And what is it exactly that you're looking for?" Candy asked frankly.

Gabby hesitated, her long list of attributes on the tip of her tongue until she realized that the eager gleam in Candy's eyes meant she was about to start committing that very list to memory, so that she could turn around and start calling every person she even vaguely knew until she could present Gabby with that perfect man, probably on a silver platter.

"Let's just say that if he walked through the door right now, I'd know it," Gabby said blandly.

As if on cue, the bells jangled, and there, in the doorway, his hair slick with rain, stood Doug Monroe.

Candy gaped at him, and Gabby felt her eyes hood. Of all the timing…

Still, she smiled brightly, making sure to keep her tone strictly professional. "Doug, nice to see you. Candy, this is Doug Monroe. We went to high school together. Doug, Candy is marrying my Uncle Dennis."

Doug shook her hand, and it wasn't lost on Gabby that as Candy set her free hand to her heart, she all but swooned.

Gabby's eyes rolled to the ceiling, but not before catching the suggestive glance that Candy slid her. A not so subtle one at that.

"My, I don't recall seeing you around town," Candy said, shifting her full attention back to Doug.

"I just moved back."

"I see." Candy blinked repeatedly. "Is your wife from these parts too?"

Oh, for heaven's sake! Gabby shook her head, refusing to take part in this spectacle.

"I'm not married," Doug said good-naturedly.

Now, Candy's eyes went wide, and she locked them on Gabby. "Is that so?"

"And he never intends to be," Gabby said firmly. "Isn't that right, Doug?"

The smile on his face slipped, and for a moment, Gabby wasn't sure if she'd said too much, embarrassed him even more than Candy was capable of doing, but he recovered quickly saying, "Married to my career, as they say."

"And what career is that?" Candy pressed.

"I'm an attorney."

Candy's eyes burst with approval again. "Is that so?"

"A divorce attorney," Gabby informed her. There. That should shut down this conversation, and any of Candy's notions.

Candy's brow pinched slightly, but still, she wasn't about to be completely deterred. "Well, I don't want to interrupt…"

"There's nothing to interrupt, Candy," Gabby said firmly. She smiled expectantly at Doug. "I'm surprised to see you back here. I know that flowers aren't exactly your favorite gift to give."

"You changed my mind about that." Doug lifted an eyebrow.

Gabby flushed with pleasure. "Glad to know I could be of service."

"Actually, the help I need today is more of a personal nature."

Candy visibly gasped and then scurried to the door. "That is most definitely my cue! Gabby I will call you later to discuss…well, you know."

Yes, Gabby did know, and she was nearly certain it had nothing to do with Candy's flowers or even Jackson Bradford. She shook her head as the door closed behind Candy, who was already pulling her phone from her bag and punching at the screen as she scurried down Main Street, not even bothering to open her umbrella.

Doug's grin was wicked as he walked to the counter and leaned into it.

Gabby folded her arms over her chest and tipped her head. "Thanks for that. In case you didn't notice, she has been trying to set me up for weeks now that she already has all of her step-daughters settled down."

"Maybe now she'll stop," Doug pointed out.

Gabby considered this. "Maybe," she said with reluctance, even though it was likely true. A single, attractive attorney had moved back to Blue Harbor. What more was there for Candy to say? On paper, he looked perfect. But Gabby knew the real Doug...At least, she thought with a start, she'd once thought she did.

"I'm here to see if you have plans this Saturday night."

Gabby blinked at him as her chest began to pound, wondering if she was hearing him correctly, if she hadn't misread their time together, if there really had been a moment on the dance floor when things shifted from an excuse to something they wanted—maybe even enjoyed.

She wondered if he was asking her on a date.

She opened her mouth and then closed it, unsure of what to say, or what she wanted to say. It was the Cherry Festival weekend; she had a solid excuse. Once upon a time, it would have been so easy. Clear cut. Black and white. The man had driven her absolutely crazy! But now... Now she had seen that there might be more to Doug than she'd first noticed.

She decided to keep things vague and friendly, because more and more, he was starting to feel like a friend. One she looked forward to seeing. One she saw a lot of, too.

"For once, I do not have a wedding to attend. Possibly my only wedding-free weekend until September."

He winced dramatically. "Unless you're willing to accompany me as my plus one?"

Her mouth was dry. *Was* this a date? What did he even mean? He'd made his stance on marriage and love as clear as the night sky. What could he possibly want from her as his plus one?

"My mom put me down with her friend's daughter," he said, raising an eyebrow. "Lanie Thompson."

Gabby felt her breath exhale. So it was a friendly favor then. Nothing more than that. She didn't know why she struggled to smile. Really, she should be relieved.

"Ah, you need a wingman, then." She knew Lanie, of course. She was attractive, a successful real estate agent, and, like Gabby, single. "Last I checked, Lanie didn't own hamsters."

Doug laughed and shook his head. "I don't want my mother thinking something might happen between us, because it won't."

She was quiet for a moment, even though a strange part of her was relieved. Many men would find the idea of a date with Lanie to be a nice way to spend the evening. "You certainly are closed off to the idea of love. Won't even give the poor girl a chance!"

He shrugged. "I'd like to say that I'm sparing her disappointment by sending the wrong message."

Gabby nodded. Perhaps it was noble of him, or perhaps it was just cynical. Either way, she should heed the advice.

"Let's just say that if you think the woman in your shop just now was pushy, she was downright tame compared to the tricks my mother is playing."

Gabby started to laugh. "Well, in that case…"

"What do you say? I know it's a big ask."

Gabby thought of the plans she had for this Saturday, or rather lack of plans altogether. In past years, her sisters and cousins had gathered together at the annual Cherry Festival, but this year, with so many of them now paired off, it wouldn't be the same. Britt would be busy running the event with Robbie, and Amelia would be selling food alongside Maddie, but this time likely with the assistance of their boyfriends Matt and Cole. Even Cora had a new man in her life, and she couldn't stop talking about showing his daughter all the wonders of the festival. Gabby had asked Jenna her plans in the hopes of pairing up together, but Jenna was busy with a summer music camp rehearsal, and her Clark cousins had bailed too. Brooke had a poetry club meeting, which Gabby was invited to, of course, not that Gabby was interested. Heidi was going on a date with a man she'd met online from a neighboring town, and Natalie couldn't find a babysitter but said Gabby was welcome to stop by her house for some drinks instead.

Then she thought of Candy's upcoming wedding, how the singles table would be filled with her cousins, possibly no longer even including Heidi, if her date this Saturday went well. There was little doubt in Gabby's mind that Candy would find a way to accommodate an extra seat and place setting for any date that any of the single ladies in the family would find at the last minute. Given that Jackson would also be at the singles table, she'd likely have to field suggestive comments and glances from Candy at every turn. Considering that Jackson and Gabby were friends,

that would be fine, if it weren't for the fact that she knew Candy would think she had triumphed, and that love was about to bloom.

The only thing blooming in Gabby's life these days were the flowers in the shop. And maybe, a friendship with Doug Monroe. It had been a long time—if ever—since she'd had such a steady male companion before, and for once, it was nice not to expect more to come from it, but rather to just enjoy his company, because that's what she was doing, she realized with a start. She actually enjoyed spending time with him.

"On one condition," Gabby said before she had a chance to consider the ramifications of her words. "You be my plus one to Candy's wedding the following Saturday."

"A family wedding?" He looked at her with such suspicion that Gabby pinched her lips, bracing herself to be put on trial, something that he had mastered at a young age.

"The worst kind," she said. "Everyone there has a vested interest in seeing me matched up. And they don't understand the kind of guy I'm looking for."

"And what kind of guy is that?" Doug asked, his voice gruff, as his eyes held hers with such interest that she eventually had to look away.

She straightened the stack of gift cards on the counter and lifted her chin a notch. "Someone attractive, at least to me. Someone kind and warm and funny. Someone who has my back and stands at my side. Someone who has passion, and interests, but makes me a priority too. Someone who is just as happy to spend a quiet night together at home as they are taking an exciting vacation. Someone who values family and this community, because I love Blue Harbor and I don't think I could ever leave. Someone who knows me and loves me for who I am, faults and all. Oh, and someone who remembers the little details. Someone who brings me my favorite flower, not because it's a holiday or birthday, but...just because."

He stared at her for an unsettling amount of time and then nodded and pulled in a breath. "Well, it sounds like you know exactly what you want. But then, you always were someone with strong opinions."

She snorted. "If that isn't the pot..."

He grinned. "Hey, we have a lot in common, including a need to get some matchmakers off our backs. So, do we have an agreement?"

He extended his hand, and she wavered for just a minute before taking it in her own. It was warm and smooth and solid, and a bolt of excitement shot up her spine.

She shook it with force, as she would in any business arrangement.

"It's a deal," she said.

He grinned at her as he pulled away. "You know, we're a lot better when we're on the same side. Some might even say a force to be reckoned with."

Gabby sighed as she watched him exit through her door and disappear down the sidewalk. It was true that she and Doug were turning out to be on the same side for many things...

Except when it came to their opinions on love and romance.

*

Doug's office was a few blocks up the street and just off Main, and the sky opened up as he pushed open the door, shuttering the loud clap of thunder.

He propped his umbrella near the coatrack and nodded to his receptionist, a nice woman named Sherry who was, like so many others, a friend of his mother who was all too happy to pick up the work since her husband had passed away last year.

"Any calls while I was gone?"

Sherry shook her head. "Your two o'clock should be here soon."

Doug nodded and gathered up the mail from the basket on her desk, pausing when he caught Sherry's watchful stare.

"Is everything okay, Sherry?" he asked.

"I was just going to ask you that."

"Me?" He looked at her quizzically.

"You look so…happy. Excuse me for saying this, but I don't think I've ever seen you quite so cheerful."

Doug didn't take the bait. He was wise enough to know that his mother had no doubt asked Sherry to do a little digging about Doug's personal life, to keep her ears open for any incoming calls from eligible women, that sort of thing.

"Huh. Must be the weather," he said with a grin as a flash of lightning made Sherry jump in her seat.

He managed not to chuckle as he walked back into his private office and settled in his chair. Did he seem happier? In truth, he felt happier. He'd kept to himself for so long that he'd forgotten how much more energized became when he got out a little and socialized.

Doug the downer. Strange that a nickname from high school could still make him frown even after all these years. Apparently, keeping his head in the books had managed to catch some people's attention anyway, even if it wasn't those that he'd hoped.

He made a mental note to take his brother up on his offer the next time Justin stopped by. Socializing was good for him, but making a habit of socializing too much with Gabby Conway was another.

He'd heard what she said, what she was looking for, and he…he couldn't promise any of those things, even if a strange part of him wanted to rise to the challenge.

Pushing away that thought, he tended to his emails, focusing on the one thing in his life he used to be able to control—work.

A short while later, Sherry tapped on his door. "Your client is here."

He pushed back his chair, standing to shake the hand of a woman who was probably only a few years older than he was. Pretty, with shoulder-length blond hair and sad blue eyes.

He saw Sherry give her the once-over, clearly assessing her potential in case it was worth reporting back to his mother. Her eyes darted away when she realized she'd been caught.

"Tea or coffee?" she asked, her cheeks flushing.

The woman held up a hand. "I'm fine, thanks."

"That will be all, Sherry," Doug said, watching patiently as his assistant reluctantly closed the door, all the way, and only after she was sure that he was still watching. A moment later he saw a red light flash on line one—no doubt Sherry was already phoning his mother with the scoop.

The client, luckily, didn't seem to pick up on this lack of professionalism and instead gave him a wary smile. "Thank you for agreeing to meet me. I...I've never done something like this before. I can't even believe I'm here."

This wasn't the first time Doug heard this. He glanced at his original correspondence with her. Married ten years. Two kids. Both seeking custody. He groaned internally.

"Please, make yourself comfortable." Once they were seated, he asked her for more details, noticing the sadness in her eyes as she explained the reason for divorce, or rather, lack thereof.

"Both of us are dedicated to the kids. But more and more, it's like we're two parents, rather than a married couple. It's not easy to find time for romance, and well, it caught up with us. It's like we're coworkers. We're not getting any younger, and I'm not sure I believe it will ever get any better, or that we can ever get back to the way it used to be." Her eyes welled with tears and he handed her a box of tissues he kept on his desk.

"Have you sought counseling?" He felt nearly as surprised at himself as the woman looked.

"Here I thought you'd just draw up the papers and get right to it!"

"I could. But I don't think that's what you want. And there's no rush." He could sense her hesitation, sense the feeling of hope that seemed to linger within her, despite the tears that she brushed away.

She nodded. "I'm almost afraid of more disappointment. That must sound cowardly." She gave him a watery smile.

He frowned at her. "It doesn't at all. You're protecting yourself. I understand."

More than she knew. Only unlike this woman, who eventually made it clear that if her husband was willing to try, she wanted their marriage to work out, Doug wasn't sure what he wanted anymore.

Or if protecting his heart at all costs was worth the price of loneliness.

10

Gabby stood outside her building on Saturday evening, staring down Main Street, only now realizing that she wasn't even sure what kind of car Doug drove, much less the color. But then, there was a lot about him that she didn't know—more than she thought. And what she had started to learn made her like him. And that…well, that wasn't necessarily a good thing.

She adjusted the heel of her strappy shoes and then smoothed down the skirt of her outfit, a dusty blue cotton lace dress that was too restrictive for the weddings where she was setting up flowers, but tonight she wouldn't have to worry about that. Tonight, she was just there to have fun. To be a wingman. A distraction.

Nothing more, she reminded herself.

Just when she was about to drop to a bench and kick off her heels, a black sedan with tinted windows came sliding down the street. She didn't need to wait for the window to roll down to know that it was Doug—the license plate made it very clear. So clear in fact that she knew she needed to get any remaining thoughts of last Saturday's dance out of her head for good. It had been a near miss. An indiscretion. A major lapse in judgment.

She bent down and glared at Doug through the open window. "Easy divorce?"

His grin made it nearly impossible to stay mad at him for long, even if years ago that grin did nothing but make her do just that. Once, she'd found it arrogant, smug even. Now she realized that Doug had a sense of humor, and getting a rise out of her was part of it.

"It was obvious? I wasn't sure from the lettering," he said.

She rolled her eyes but resisted the grin that was tugging at her mouth as she opened the door and slid onto the smooth leather seat. "Oh, it was obvious." Glaring, really. A reminder that she needed to get her emotions in check and pronto. This man was just as much trouble as Jackson Bradford, possibly worse. And just like Jackson, he would remain a friend.

An attractive friend, she thought, quickly raking her eyes over him. So he filled out a suit nicely. Plenty of men did.

He shrugged. "You're a business owner. It's marketing."

"It's crass," she replied, clicking her seat belt in place. She gave him a scolding look, but his gaze had already drifted to her legs. Stiffening, she set her handbag on her lap. Her pulse began to race.

"So…how is business?" Not that she particularly wanted to know about all the broken hearts in town, but it was conversation, and this was a little awkward, sitting here in his car, while he merged with the steady but light flow of traffic and began to move down the familiar streets that she had walked and biked a thousand times, even if now they felt a little different. She hadn't been in a car with a man in…too long to admit. It felt exciting. And that was something that she really couldn't afford to feel. Not with a man who had chosen a license plate like that, even if it was probably just in jest.

"It will take time to build my practice up," he said.

"Not enough people falling out of love?" She met his sidelong glance and managed to suppress a grin.

"Believe it or not, I'm trying to help people." He glanced at her, and despite her reservation, she shrugged.

"But to answer your question, I'm branching out into other towns. Blue Harbor is small. There are only so many people who could ever require my services."

She nodded, understanding the need to expand the scope of marketing. "Several of my customers come from Pine Falls, especially for big events. But the deliveries for everyday celebrations are usually people in Blue Harbor."

"Any idea who is doing the flowers for tonight's wedding?" he asked.

"No, but I'll admit I'm curious. Almost as curious to know how it is you managed to get a plus one so close to the wedding. The bride and groom don't mind?"

He gave her a little wince. "They didn't do a table chart."

She gasped, unsure what was more horrifying, that guests would be left to sit wherever they could find a chair or that she was essentially crashing the party.

"Please tell me you told them I was coming." Her next sentence would be to tell him to turn the car around, or to let her out at the corner. She could walk back.

He laughed then, a long and throaty laugh that made her start to snicker, even though she didn't see what was so funny.

"Oh, you should have seen the look on your face!" He wiped his eyes at the next intersection, still chuckling.

Her gaze hooded. "I see that weddings and marriage are all fun and games to you."

He made a big show of sobering his expression. "And they are clearly serious business to you!" He shook his head. "Aren't weddings supposed to be fun?"

"That's an interesting comment coming from you. I seem to recall you saying that you'd rather be home than sitting at a reception table, toasting to the happy couple."

He gave her a wry look. "I meant that the wedding is the fun part."

"Let me guess," she said drolly. "It's what comes afterward that is less fun."

He held up a palm. "You said it, not me."

She could only shake her head. "They *do* know I'm coming?"

"Yes, they know you're coming. My mother, on the other hand…" His brows shot up, and now it was her turn to laugh. She looked through the window as they came to the park, just at the edge of town. It was another outdoor wedding, and while the sky had been overcast that morning, the rain had held off so far.

A string quartet could be heard as they walked across the grass to where the guests were already seated for the ceremony. Gabby watched Mrs. Monroe's eyes widen when she saw Doug and then Gabby, but Doug's expression remained unchanged when he dropped into the seat behind his parents and said, "Mom, you remember my friend Gabby Conway."

Carol's smile was even larger than it had been when she'd thanked Gabby for the birthday arrangement. "Of course, Gabby, so nice to see you here!"

It was painfully obvious that there was much more that Mrs. Monroe wanted to say, but she pinched her lips firmly. "It seems that we're often at the same places these days." Here her eyes drifted to her son.

Doug remained expressionless as he pulled the ribbon from the program and unrolled it.

"Yes, well, it is wedding season," Gabby said with a smile. "I have a wedding booked nearly every weekend through September, I think."

"Oh, this is the last one for us," Carol said. She again glanced at Doug, who pretended to be extremely engrossed in the music and reading selections for tonight's ceremony. "Isn't your uncle getting married soon?"

"Next weekend," Gabby confirmed. And it couldn't come soon enough. All week she'd been fielding calls from her cousins about Candy's latest demands and ideas, and with mild reluctance, had agreed to attend the last fitting for their bridesmaid dresses this coming week. She supposed Brooke wouldn't mind the buffer, either. Every time Candy walked into Something Blue, she spotted a new gown that made her doubt her own. But then, Gabby understood. She couldn't step into her sister's boutique without wanting to try every dress on, too.

The music swelled, signaling the start of the ceremony, and Mrs. Monroe fell quiet as everyone turned to watch. The mother of the groom was first down the aisle, dressed in a lovely peach dress that rustled in the breeze, led to her seat by the groom's brother. Gabby caught Carol's look of longing before she relaxed back against her chair.

Gabby slid a discreet look at Doug, who gave her a subtle but conspiratorial wink as they stood for the bride. Gabby didn't know her—the family was from a neighboring town—and just for tonight, she felt like she could relax into the event, and not fret over the flowers or the weather or the fear of disappointing the bride.

She glanced at Doug and they exchanged a small smile.

And just for a moment, Gabby almost forgot that this wasn't a real date.

*

"Well, I can tell you didn't do the flowers," Doug whispered to Gabby as they walked down the slope to the tent where the reception was being held next to the duck pond.

She looked up at him in surprise, her green eyes flashing as her grin turned wary. "And how is that?"

He jutted his chin to the tables, where large vases held flowers that he could never name, well, maybe aside from the roses. "These have a lot of greenery, whereas your arrangements always show off the flowers themselves."

"I can't believe you noticed that," she said softly.

135

His stare bore down on hers. "I notice a lot of things about you."

Her cheeks turned pink when she blinked, and he cleared his throat, squaring his shoulders and looking away. He thrust his hands in his pockets, focusing on the party they were joining. "Makes it easier to tease you."

She gave him a playful swat, pulling his attention back to her. "You certainly do seem to make a sport of that. Why is that?"

He stiffened, knowing the answer wasn't one he wasn't willing to share and for once at a loss of words for how to make another excuse for his behavior. Before he had a chance to answer, a look of recognition seemed to pass through her eyes and her cheeks turned a shade redder. She broke his stare, looking around at the various tables. "I...I think I need a glass of champagne. What's a wedding without it?" She gave a laugh that sounded as nervous as he felt.

He grabbed two flutes of champagne from a passing waiter and held one to her. "I'd suggest we find our table, but it looks like we have our pick. Should we claim our spots early?"

"Before we get stuck sitting with your parents, you mean?"

He grinned. "Exactly." It was refreshing, this easy conversation they had, and enjoyable too. Not quite as fun as working her up, seeing her lips pinch and her eyes blaze as she was prone to do back in high school, but as she had pointed out, they weren't in high school anymore. They'd grown up. And she had grown even more beautiful.

He let her lead the way, her long hair grazing her bare back as she finally stopped at a table closest to the pond. "I just love weeping willows," she sighed.

He wasn't aware that he was staring at her until her brow pinched and she said, "Let me guess. You have fifteen facts up your sleeve for why I should not love that particular kind of tree."

He decided to humor her. It was easier to fall back on their old dynamic. Safer too. Back then it had been a way to guard his heart. Something he'd lost sight of in recent weeks.

"And what is it about a drooping, sad-looking tree that makes you love it so much?" he asked as they slipped into their seats at a table with two other couples, both slightly older than they were and likely out-of-town guests.

She just shook her head at him and gave a little smile. "They're so romantic."

Well, she had managed to officially silence him there. He glanced over at the pond in the distance, at the eaves that were grazing the water's surface, and then back to the girl sitting beside him, who was casually sipping her champagne with one hand, brushing a loose strand of hair off her neck with the other.

The last two seats of their table were soon filled, and introductions were made. Doug didn't bother to glance around the tent to see where his mother was sitting—he didn't need to. He could feel her stare from three tables over, sense it in his periphery.

He told himself she just wanted the best for him. Wanted him to settle down, find the kind of love and life that she and his father had. They made it look so easy, but he knew better than that.

With a large smile, he waved directly at his mother, who looked a little startled by being caught. She gave a hesitant smile, then a very obvious look at Gabby. Let her believe what she would. At least for tonight, she could think her job was complete.

He turned back to the table. It was quickly established that, as he'd assumed, everyone else at the table was married, and, it would seem, happily so.

"And how long have you two been together?" one woman asked once the main course had been brought to the table.

Gabby turned to him with wide eyes, as if expecting him to take this one, and he could have sworn he saw a flash of amusement pass through them. He supposed he deserved it.

"Gabby and I both grew up in Blue Harbor," he said. Nothing dishonest there. "We really connected with the debate club, though."

He gave her a challenging look, fighting off the twitch in his lips.

"Debate club?" This seemed to pique the interest of a few of their tablemates.

"I thought it would be good practice for law school," Doug said. "But I don't think I ever knew why you joined, Gabby."

Her cheeks reddened and she didn't meet his eye as she reached for her wineglass. "I overheard a guy I had a crush on mention that he planned to join the club. I joined, he did not. And the rest, as they say, is history."

Doug peered at her, as the table gave a collective laugh, seeming to find this amusing.

"I learn something new about you every day," he marveled in a low voice. "Chad's loss was my gain."

"Are you saying that debate club would have been less interesting if I wasn't there?"

"Without a doubt." He gave her a slow smile, sensing something growing between them, and felt a strange mix of enjoyment and wariness. "Oh, look. They're cutting the cake. I know that's your favorite part."

She elbowed him. "You know me too well."

He did. And everything new he learned was one more thing to like about her. And that was just the problem. Back in high school, a girl like Gabby wouldn't have given him a second glance—like the rest, she had eyes for the jocks and the jerks. And now…now he wondered if she would, if he was willing.

When the toasts were finished and the cake was passed around, he said to her, "What do you say we take these plates and go look at the weeping willow trees you love so much?" He lowered his voice, leaning in to whisper in her ear. "Between you and me, I can literally feel my mother's eyes boring a hole through me right now. If I don't move my neck to the left soon, I'm afraid I'm going to wake up with a kink in it."

She laughed and quietly took her plate and fork, following him down the grass until they were finally hidden by the trees.

"Why is it exactly that your mother is so determined to set you up? Is she afraid you won't stay in Blue Harbor otherwise?"

"I love Blue Harbor. I missed it when I was away. I don't see myself leaving again."

From the little smile she gave, she seemed to like that answer.

"No, the real reason is that she's worried about me. She doesn't think I'm happy, and she thinks the only reason I came back to Blue Harbor is to run away from love."

gabby stopped at the bench under the tree and narrowed her eyes on him. "Wait. Are you telling me that you've been in love?"

He considered this statement. He tended to take words at their value, and this was a topic he didn't feel he could expertly argue.

"To be honest, I don't think I can answer that question." He shrugged. "I thought I was in love at the time. Now…now I'm not so sure."

She dropped onto the bench dramatically. "And here I thought you didn't believe in love."

He managed a rueful grin and took the space beside her. "Your debate skills are paying off. Your word choice has me on the spot."

"So do you? Believe in love, that is?"

He wasn't going to let her off that easily. Besides, it was too broad a question to answer. Even to himself. "In general, or for me personally?"

"For you personally," she said, and he raised an eyebrow, surprised that she was this interested in his personal life and not just in having an argument. But then, something had shifted between them these last few weeks, something had maybe even grown. Gone were the days of being right for the sheer sake of it. Now, he preferred to be understood.

"It's not very easy to measure an emotion, is it?"

She gave a slow nod of her head, looking far too entertained for his liking. He had the uneasy feeling that he was losing this debate, and that for once, she was the one who was doing the gloating at making him squirm.

"Ah, I see, we're back to the evidence now. I know for a fact that love exists, and that it lasts," Gabby said.

"I won't bother to argue with you," he said, because the truth was that he agreed with her. Love did exist, and for the lucky ones, it also lasted. There was no doubt in his mind that his parents would be together forever, that when he saw his mother reach over and take his father's hand, it was with just as much, if not more, love than they'd had for each other on their wedding day.

He felt a pull in his stomach when he thought of his own circumstances.

"So then by agreeing with me, you're also saying that you do believe in love." The smug satisfaction in her smile was so cute that he felt his eyes linger a moment longer than he should.

Clearing his throat, he looked away, watching the ducks bob in the water, occasionally dipping their heads below the tranquil surface.

"Fine. I do believe in love. For others."

Her brow knitted. "Why not for yourself?"

He leaned back against the bench, releasing a pent-up breath. "I was engaged before I came here."

Now she set her fork down and gaped at him. "Douglas Monroe. You mean to tell me that you, the man who doesn't believe in happy endings, actually did something as romantic as propose to a woman?"

There was no getting out of this one. He shoveled a piece of cake into his mouth. A little drier than last weekend's cake. By now he could almost become a wedding critic.

He supposed in many ways, he already was one.

"Down on one knee, with a ring and everything."

Her eyes were wide as she continued to stare at him with an open mouth of surprise. "But that's just so...so optimistic of you!"

"I was a different man back then," he said, shrugging.

She looked at him sadly and returned to her cake, going for the icing first, like last time. "What happened? If you don't mind me asking."

"I'm the one who volunteered the information. The topic is free game now." He set his plate in his lap. "We were halfway through the planning, and then one day she just said that she didn't want to do it anymore. That she didn't love me. And that maybe she never had."

"Ouch." Gabby winced. "And you didn't see it coming?"

He let out a laugh that bore no amusement. "No, I didn't. Now, looking back, I can see that things hadn't been right between us for a while. That maybe they'd never been right. We were colleagues, and we had our work in common. We had a lot in common, really. We seemed like such a good fit, but something was missing. Something I can't put into words. A feeling, in the gut."

She looked pensive for a moment. "I think I know what you mean," she said quietly. "Someone can look so right on paper, and sometimes, someone can look so wrong, but your heart says otherwise."

He held her eyes for a beat and then looked away. He'd divulged too much already. Shared more than he had with anyone in a long time, maybe ever.

"Well," he said, shrugging off the old injury. "Now you know my little secret."

"And I'm guessing it's the reason why your mother is so determined to see you matched up and soon."

"She assumes I'm lonely, which I'm not." Only that wasn't completely true. He wasn't lonely tonight, sitting beside Gabby. If anything, he'd dare to say that he was perfectly content in a way he had never been with Lisa. "And she thinks that if I find the right woman that I'll be happier." He shook his head. "It's not that easy."

"Maybe it is," Gabby countered. "I mean, look at the bride and groom. And my cousins, and even my sister. I'm not saying that they didn't have setbacks or stumbles, but a lot of it was about being in the same place at the same time. Being ready. When it clicks, it clicks."

"When it clicks, it clicks." He looked at her, feeling a pull rise up that was stronger than anything he could push aside. It was the feeling, deep inside, the one that had nothing to do with ration or reason or facts or the promise he'd made to himself, either. It was bigger than that, irrefutable, even if it couldn't be proven or factored in as evidence. It was reckless, the kind of emotion that led people to make the wrong choices, to end up in his office years or months later, tearful and disappointed, broken or angry.

Only right now, he didn't feel any of those things. And all those little warnings that told him to stand up, walk away, call it a night and go home, were replaced with something deeper and stronger, and so much better.

His eyes locked with hers, and he could feel his breathing slow as his heart started to pound. She was so close, and so beautiful, and it would be so easy to lean forward and kiss her right now. It was what he wanted. It was also, he supposed, what he feared. Following this feeling, daring to believe that it wouldn't lead him astray. That he too could be one of the lucky ones.

A burst of applause erupted from the tent, pulling Gabby's attention from his. She turned, looking at the commotion, and said, "They're going to toss the bouquet."

He looked at her, seeing the hope that filled her eyes when she looked back at him, and he knew that he couldn't even find it in himself to tease her for this, even though once it would have been so easy.

"Go on then. Maybe you'll catch it."

She waggled her eyebrows and set down her cake. He watched from the bench as she hurried up the grass to the small fountain near the tent where the women were gathered, the bride holding the bouquet high in the air, and he found himself hoping that Gabby would be the one to catch the bouquet, and not just because it would make her happy.

He'd seen that hope in her eyes, the belief that love would find a way into her life, and a part of him couldn't help but want to find that for himself, too.

11

Gabby sat in one of the blush-colored velvet chairs in the center of Brooke's shop, covering her mouth with her hand while Candy silently flipped through the bridal lookbook, "just in case she missed something."

She didn't dare look up and catch her sister's eye. Every time she did, Brooke's wide-eyed stare made her nearly burst out laughing, and more than once Gabby had needed to excuse herself to the bathroom.

The wedding was now only three days away, meaning that there was no more time for any changes. Today was meant to be the final fitting.

"Everything is just so beautiful." Candy sighed and finally closed the book.

Brooke wasted no time in bending forward and taking it from the table. She disappeared without a word into her back room, hugging it close to her chest. Candy sipped her tea and looked over to the dressing rooms, where the four daughters of Uncle Dennis were changing into their bridesmaid dresses.

"I'm sorry I didn't get here in time to see you in your gown, Candy," Gabby said. A last-minute sympathy order had kept her at the shop longer than she'd planned. "But I guess it won't be long now before I see you walk down the aisle in it."

"Oh, enough about me." Candy leaned in closer. "Who was that handsome man that was in your shop last week?"

Gabby knew this was coming, and she'd prepared for it, only now, she wondered if Candy would see through the lack of conviction in her protest.

"What handsome man?" Britt asked, coming out of the dressing room. She was in a carnation-pink chiffon dress that flowed from the waist and stopped just below the knee. It was simple and elegant and captured Brooke's design style, which had been honed when she worked for a major designer in New York.

Gabby was just a little surprised that Candy hadn't managed to convince Brooke to go for something a little more…noticeable.

"Ah, this fits perfectly," Brooke said now, looking much more relaxed as she emerged from the back room, without her lookbook. She pinched at the fabric near Britt's waist and had her turn in front of the three-way mirror. "Lovely, isn't it, Candy?"

Her tone left no room for argument. Gabby pressed her lips closed to ward off a smile. She didn't dare meet her cousin's eye. The other three girls seemed to be hiding in their dressing rooms, letting Britt, as the eldest, deal with Candy's final opinion.

Final was a very vague word in Candy's vocabulary.

"It's very pretty. I do remember loving the big, ruffled collar—"

"We discussed that, though, Candy, remember?" Brooke gave her a polite smile, but Gabby was able to detect the tension in her jaw. "You don't want anyone to outshine the bride!"

This seemed to perk Candy up and she nodded eagerly. "No, we wouldn't want that." She let out a sigh and then gave a quick nod of consent. "It's perfect."

"Good, now that that's settled, who is this handsome man Candy is referring to?" Britt raised an eyebrow in question as her sisters emerged from the dressing room in identical gowns looking both relieved and eager to be part of the conversation as it was unfolding.

Brooke snapped a look of curiosity in Gabby's direction before turning her attention to Cora, who was directed to stand in front of the mirror while Brooke pinned her hem.

"Doug Monroe is back in town," Gabby explained to the girls, even though Maddie was fully aware, and Candy had probably told Amelia all about him in the kitchen of the café. "He's an old friend," she insisted to Candy, even though she wasn't exactly sure that was true. Friends didn't try to kiss each other, and that's exactly what she had felt Doug was about to do on Saturday night.

A part of her was still disappointed that he hadn't, until she reminded herself of where he stood on all the points she valued most.

On the opposing side. Like always.

"He is quite handsome," Candy gave her a pointed look. "And single."

"Unmarried," Gabby corrected. It was hardly the same thing as single, not that she felt like explaining this to Candy or giving her further cause to read into things.

"Why was he in the shop?" Maddie asked, her eyes gleaming with interest.

"Friendly visit." Immediately sensing that this had only piqued everyone's interest, including Brooke, who had stopped pinning for a moment, Gabby added, "And I do sell flowers, as you remember." Not that he had purchased any. No, his visit was just that. Friendly. Maybe even personal. "We're friends. That's all it is."

Candy wasn't buying it any more than the others. "You say the same thing about Jackson but I see the way you two banter." She crossed one leg over the other and said airily, "Just in case you have a change of heart, I've left a little wiggle room in the seating chart."

She still hadn't told Candy that she was bringing Doug, and now that grand plan was starting to feel like a bad idea, and not just because Candy would read way too far into it. Sure, it might help her to drop the idea that Gabby and Jackson were a perfect match, but it might make her start thinking about planning Gabby's wedding next, and sadly, that wasn't going to happen, and not just because she was yet to catch a bridal bouquet, only create them.

After all, Doug didn't believe he could find love, didn't believe in trying to make it last for the long term. Wasn't willing to put his heart on the line again.

And she knew better than to try to change people or expect to transform him. If she'd had that attitude, she would have tried to transform Jackson years ago.

Except... She brushed that thought aside but it kept nagging at her. Except that Jackson had never gotten to her the way that Doug had, or did. With Jackson, she was distanced, objective, and with Doug, it was all emotion, and she never did get to a rational place when it came to him.

All the more reason to try to do that now.

"Well, if you're going to insist that you're just friends, then maybe I should tell you..."

Gabby stared at her future aunt in dread. She should have known Candy wouldn't let this topic rest. "Tell me what, Candy? What did you do?"

Her cousins took that as their cue to scamper back into the dressing rooms. Gabby flashed a pleading look at Brooke, but she was too busy smothering a laugh and muttered some excuse before dashing into the back room. No doubt they'd all be eavesdropping from a safe distance.

"Well, when you insisted on coming to the wedding alone, I made a few calls."

Oh, brother. "A few calls? Oh, Candy, tell me you didn't call Jackson!"

"No, no, I see what you mean about that young man. I do think there is hope for him, but I agree, not with you."

"Gee, thanks." Gabby almost laughed.

"I was just calling the people who hadn't yet responded to the invitation," Candy started to explain quickly, "and I got to chatting with one of my old summer friends. They have a house over on the island, you see. She was a bit older than me, but we kept in touch over the years, not as much as I would have liked, but then, she did the married with kids thing, and I... Well, in many ways, I was like you, Gabby. Waiting for the right man."

Gabby didn't know whether to feel touched or fearful, considering that Candy was hardly in the prime of her youth and her Uncle Dennis had four adult daughters from his first marriage. But here was Candy, the happiest bride she'd ever met, even if she was also the pickiest. It was the day she had been waiting for all her life, and it was finally almost here.

And nothing that Candy could say now would make Gabby ruin it for her.

"And then I remembered that she had a son who was just a touch older than you. Turns out he is a doctor!"

Gabby threw herself back in her chair. "A doctor with a pregnant wife on bed rest with kids?"

Candy looked stricken. "No! A doctor with a private practice in Pine Falls. I'll admit that I haven't seen a photo despite some internet research, but his mother was always a beauty."

Gabby groaned. "Candy..."

Candy held up a hand. "Now, you might not even like him. I didn't screen him as much as I would have liked..."

Gabby heard giggling from somewhere in the dressing rooms.

Candy, however, didn't seem to notice. She sipped her tea and, after a dramatic pause, glanced at Gabby. "I did seat him at the singles table rather than with his parents. I can change it, of course. Though I really can't even imagine changing *anything* at the final hour like this..."

Gabby stared at Candy in disbelief, managing to keep from bursting out laughing, and for a moment she was happy that Brooke had left her to fend for herself. Surely Brooke wouldn't have been able to keep quiet after this afternoon.

"Actually, Candy, I might bring Doug after all." There, it was out.

Candy's eyes went round, and she didn't even try to hide her smile. "So something *is* going on between the two of you. Of course, it will be no trouble to fit him in!" Suddenly, her expression folded and she brought her fist to her mouth. "Oh, but then, there's Billy to consider…"

Or not. The last thing Gabby needed was to spend the duration of Candy's wedding being set up on a blind date. It would mean awkward, forced interaction, and all under Candy's watchful gaze.

"Maybe he'll be a good match for one of the Clark girls," Gabby offered.

"Or maybe he'll be a good match for you." Candy shrugged. "Having two men vying for your affection is certainly a fine position to be in, don't you think?"

Gabby could only shake her head. What difference did it make if a random single man was seated at her table? Once this might have excited her, made her worry about her hair and her dress and even her table manners. But now she'd learned not to pin so much hope on these events.

It was so much easier to be herself and enjoy the event. And lately, she'd been able to do just that…thanks to Doug.

*

Doug decided that meeting up with his brother was better than sitting home. Besides, he was out of frozen dinners, and he suspected that if he called one of the local pizza places again, they'd recite his order without him having to give it, and that was just too embarrassing to think about right now. And one of the downsides of coming back to this town.

The upsides were numerous, though. And sliding onto a stool at a high top at Harrison's Pub that night across from his brother was proof of that.

"You didn't want to go to the Carriage House?" Justin glanced around the room. "No girls here."

"Exactly," Doug said over his menu. Harrison's was the kind of place you came for a beer and a burger, to catch the game, and maybe shoot a game of pool. He was at no risk of running into Gabby Conway here, though not for the reasons he might have once thought. Back in the day, he'd have assumed a pretty girl like Gabby would have turned her nose at a place like this. Now, he could almost picture her throwing a few darts, getting into the spirit of competition.

The thought must have made him smile because Justin was looking at him strangely from across the table.

"You think you're going to find a wife hiding out in a place like this?"

Doug snorted into his beer. "Why does my entire family think I need a wife?"

"You were open to the idea of marriage once before," Justin pointed out. "I assumed you were ready to settle down."

"Settling down means finding the right person," Doug said firmly. "Besides, I don't see you dating anyone seriously."

Justin shrugged. "We're not talking about me. And you know Mom will move on to me once she's through with you."

Now Doug laughed. "In that case, I'll take my sweet time. You owe me one."

"Well, she's certainly happy you're home. She told me that was her best birthday gift, having you there."

"Better than my gift card?" Doug set the menu to the side and looked over his shoulder to where Ryan Harrison was taking drink orders at the bar.

"Gift card?" Justin tutted.

"What? I thought she'd like that, to treat herself…"

"Oh, Doug. For my older brother, you have a lot to learn about women. They like the personal touch."

Doug raised his eyebrows. A few months ago, he might have thought that this was where things went off-track with Lisa—they'd been so in sync when it came to how they planned each day that he hadn't stopped to make sweeping gestures, something he later regretted. Now, though, he knew that there was more to it than that. He just wished he could be sure it wouldn't happen again.

"You're frowning." Justin cursed under his breath. "Sorry, I didn't mean to insult your gift. I'm sure Mom loved it, especially with all the weddings she's been invited to lately. Gave her an excuse to get her hair and nails done."

"No, it was something else." Doug shook away the cobwebs, relieved when Ryan came over to take their orders.

"The place is looking good," Justin told him, handing over his menu.

Ryan shrugged, but he looked pleased. "If you'd asked me a year ago what I'd be doing right now, I can tell you that I never would have said I'd be back in Blue Harbor running my late father's bar, but I've never been happier."

"What made you decide to come back to town?" Doug asked. He recalled from their school days that Ryan had planned to pursue a degree in business or accounting—something like that.

"Honestly? Bad breakup." Ryan shook his head.

Justin raised an eyebrow at Doug, who did his best to ignore it. "Seeing anyone now?"

Ryan clicked the top of his pen and shook her head. "Nah. The only women I seem to see much of these days are my mother and my sister-in-law. And Brooke's sister, too."

Doug suspected that he wasn't referring to the youngest of the Conway sisters. He knew that Brooke and Gabby were close, and even though Ryan hadn't inferred that anything was happening between the two of them, he felt a strange flare of jealousy.

Justin gave him a teasing look over the table when Ryan moved on to the next table. "Sound familiar? Only sounds to me like he's open to finding love again." Justin, like his mother, didn't seem to want to let this drop.

"Good for him." Doug swigged his beer. Just so long as it wasn't with Gabby Conway.

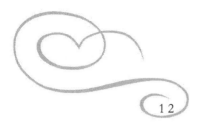

12

Gabby finished tucking the last stem into her arrangement and stepped back to admire it. It was a happy mix of flowers in shades of pink, white, orange, purple, and yellow. It was just about right, but only just. She tapped a finger against her mouth; something was missing, now to decide what exactly it was...

With a grin, she picked up a few more stems of snapdragons and carefully placed them between the other flowers. There. Now it was perfect.

And late! She glanced at the clock in panic as she hurried to untie her apron strings. She was always prone to losing time when she was arranging. It was her happiest task of the day, selecting each flower, thinking of how it would pair with the others, trying to keep the designs interesting. But the most fulfilling part of the job was the delivery. Her mother wasn't helping today, and that meant that Gabby was on her own, and she'd promised to get this out right after the shop closed. Technically the shop had closed fifteen minutes ago; she just hadn't stopped to turn the sign on the door.

Now, she cleaned her workspace, prepped the flowers for tomorrow, and flicked the lights before turning the sign and locking the door with one hand while carefully holding the arrangement with another.

She hurried along Main Street, dodging tourists who had made an early start on the weekend and seasonal visitors who came when school let out each summer and stayed through until the end of August. She kept her pace steady, weaving between a man on a bicycle and a child holding an ice cream cone, but she slowed her pace when she saw Doug Monroe stepping out of his office on the corner, with a woman.

Holding the arrangement a little higher to hide her face, she quietly neared, trying to gather a snippet of their conversation as she peeked through the petals. The woman was pretty, not much older than herself, and Doug walked her to the curb, where she unlocked her car. He said something that made her laugh, and she waved him goodbye before climbing into the sedan and quickly pulling away.

Doug pushed his hands into his pockets and watched her go and then, before Gabby had a chance to turn around and run the other way, he turned and looked right at her.

Or at least, right at the giant arrangement.

He narrowed his eyes in suspicion, barely fighting off a grin as he tipped his head from side to side, trying to determine if that was her, even though she was fairly sure this much was obvious.

"Gabby?"

She pulled the arrangement down too quickly, nearly whipping her face with an iris.

"Oh, hey, Doug. I didn't see you there!" She gave an internal eye roll; that was hardly smooth, or convincing, judging by the lift of his eyebrow.

"You finished for the day?"

She nodded and adjusted the vase in her hands. "Last delivery."

"Here, let me help you," he said, lifting the arrangement from her hands before she could refuse.

Her hands felt lighter already as she righted the handbag straps on her shoulder. "Thanks. It's just a few blocks over."

"Lead the way." He fell into step beside her, and Gabby used the opportunity to double-check the exact address on the order form.

"So," she said when she'd tucked the order sheet back into her bag. "You're done for the day too?"

He gave her a look that told her he saw through her lame effort for polite conversation. "Just walked my last client out."

"Oh, a client!" She swallowed back the excitement in her voice. Really, who cared if she had just seen Doug with an attractive woman? "I'm surprised," she added, covering her emotion.

"Surprised?"

"Well, she looked...so happy, I guess." Shoot. Now he'd know for sure that she'd noticed him earlier.

He raised a knowing eyebrow. "You assume that everyone who seeks my services is miserable."

She gave a little wince. "I suppose so."

"Believe it or not, sometimes it's better to be alone than in a bad relationship."

Gabby considered this. "I guess you're right." She jutted her chin to the white house on the corner. It was one of the smaller inns in town, a little more rundown than the larger ones on Main Street. "This is my stop."

She went to reach for the arrangement, but Doug simply pushed open the picket fence gate bearing a welcome sign and said, "After you."

"Ah, you want to see how it's done, do you?"

"I suppose I'm equally curious about your career," he said.

She decided to feel flattered by that and took the stairs to the front porch and tried the door. Inside the small reception area, it was dark but cozy, and a woman with shoulder-length blond hair greeted them in surprise. Gabby vaguely knew her; she'd been a few years below her sister Jenna in school and this inn had been passed down from her parents.

"You have a delivery," Gabby said with a smile.

The young woman's face lit up as she stared at the flowers that Doug handed to her. "Oh my! For me?"

Her eyes welled with tears as she set the vase down and searched amongst the flowers for the card that Gabby had written earlier. Gabby, of course, already knew what it said. It was from her husband, who had been deployed overseas for one year as of today.

"Oh, this is the best thing I've seen all day. All week!" She held the card to her chest and smiled broadly at Gabby and Doug. "Thank you so much!"

Gabby shrugged. She was just the messenger, but she liked to still think she played a small part in this moment.

Doug waited until they were outside on the porch again to say, "Was it her birthday?"

"Nope. Not a special occasion, per se. But sometimes people just need to know they're in someone's thoughts." She sighed happily, only frowning slightly when she caught Doug staring at her intensely.

"It must feel good, making people happy all the time."

"Or at least cheering them up," Gabby said, thinking of the sympathy bouquets she made. "But yes, it does feel good to know that I played a small part in making someone's day a little better."

"I guess I never thought about it like that."

"So I've enlightened you?" She gave him a lock of mock surprise that pulled a grin out of him.

"In more ways than you know," he said in a low voice, and then cleared his throat. They walked another half a block before he spoke again. "What are you doing with the rest of your evening?"

Gabby felt her heart speed up, not sure what he meant by this. "Oh, I might take a walk near the lake. I've been cooped up all day."

"Mind some company?" he asked.

She fought back a smile. "Not at all."

*

They walked down the gravel path to the lakefront, where already the sounds of children splashing in the water could be heard in the near distance.

Gabby laughed. "The water is still cold this time of year."

"Never stopped me before," Doug said, dropping onto a large rock to start removing his shoes. He gave her an expectant look, and she shook her head.

"Oh no. I wait until at least August. I'm not a little kid anymore. The cold bothers me now."

"Come on, now. You can at least dip your feet in."

He had her there. She was wearing sandals, too, which were easy enough to slip off. She opened her bag to tuck them inside, pushing aside her latest paperback so she wouldn't dirty the pages, finally deciding to set the book on top of her bag.

"No splashing," she warned. She wouldn't put it past him.

"No worries. I just planned to dunk you." She shook her head ruefully, that was until he made a grab for her book. "The Rogue—" he started, and then stopped when she yanked it from his grip.

"Hey!"

His eyes twinkled with amusement, and there was laughter in his voice. "I was just wondering what could be so captivating about this book that you would carry it around with you."

"I like to have a book with me," she replied defensively.

"For escaping into a more romantic world when the urge arises?"

She narrowed her eyes at him, but he was grinning wider. "Very funny. Actually...actually, I find that it's nice to have a book in case I grab a coffee or stop by the bakery."

His expression changed, sobering a little. He stepped down into the water, nodding. "For when you're alone and no one else is." He glanced at her over his shoulder. "I get it. I used to do that back in high school, only back then, I was also genuinely more interested in studying, or at least, I thought I had to be."

She hadn't ever thought of it so literally before, but he was right. When she was sitting in the café or bakery, by herself, it helped to have a book on hand, something to keep her occupied, something to give her an excuse to not be with someone. As for her choice of genre, she couldn't deny that she liked to believe that romance was possible.

Maybe, she thought, glancing at Doug, even for her.

"I don't mind being alone," she said a little defensively. "I just…think my life would be more fulfilling with someone in it."

She glanced at him as she waded into the cool water, which wasn't nearly as icy as she'd expected it to be at this point in the summer.

"Not bad, eh?"

"Rather nice," she admitted, wiggling her toes in the sand.

"But these rogues," he started again, and she swatted him on the arm as he erupted in laughter. "I'm sorry, I'm sorry," he begged her off, still sputtering on his amusement. "I just…I don't think I know exactly what a rogue is."

She pursed her lips. "You're making fun of me again."

His gaze softened. "I'm not making fun of you. I'm just…curious about you. And you have to admit that you're easy to tease."

Gabby sucked in a breath, thinking of what her cousin Bella had said, or had it been Brooke? Or both of them? Doug had always singled her out in prom committee and debate club. At the time, she'd assumed it was because he didn't like her, but now she wondered…

She brushed aside that theory. No. Doug had made every interaction downright miserable. Until lately.

"I suppose I should be grateful that you're only making fun of my reading selections and not my career choice," she said.

"I meant what I said today," Doug said, serious now. "It's special what you do, Gabby. You have a real impact on someone's life in a positive way."

"Oh, well, I'm not out saving lives, but I enjoy it. It really inspires me to share what I love."

He nodded, growing quiet, and she realized she had just said the L-word again. Was it any wonder no men were asking her out these days? She probably scared them off with all her talk of romance and flowers and love.

"No wonder you were so particular about the centerpieces in prom committee," he said, giving her a knowing look.

"Hey, I'm still mad at you about rejecting my snow globe theme for the Winter Wonderland prom."

"Can I make a confession? I really liked that idea."

She stared at him. She could still remember how excited she had been to present it to the group and how furious she had been when he claimed he couldn't quite picture it.

"I had to defend my vision with a forty-minute speech along with visuals and a sample!" she all but screeched, even though he was laughing, and she was too. Sort of. "Why would you put me through that if you liked the concept?"

He pulled a face, as if he knew he was in trouble. "I liked seeing you explain it. You were so passionate and excited, and determined."

Oh. She stepped back, deeper into the water, drawing a circle through the waves with her foot. "I guess I always knew what I wanted to do, even back then."

"I know," he said.

"Well, the same goes for you," she said. "You always wanted to go to college and then law school."

"I did," he said, nodding pensively. "And I needed a scholarship to do it. I wanted to go into family law. And I did."

She frowned. "But you're a divorce attorney now. Why the change?"

"It's a natural transition," he said slowly, "but...after my engagement ended, I guess I felt better suited to it."

Huh. She waded through the water until she reached the shore, and then dropped down onto the dry sand, careful not to splash her book which was still resting nearby on the rock. "You wanted to help people who felt the same way you did."

She felt ashamed to think that she'd given him such a hard time, assumed his motive had been cynical, or even bitter.

"To be honest, you were right about another thing. For the most part, people in this town are pretty happy. I'm…well, I'm thinking of broadening the scope of practice." He dropped onto the sand beside her, close enough that his arm brushed hers. She didn't back away and he didn't seem to feel the need to shift, either.

"Guess that means you'll have to get a new license plate," she said, lightening the tension that was building within her.

He laughed. "Maybe you can help me think of a better one."

She pulled in a breath, locking his gaze, and looked away quickly. Their last scheduled wedding was this Saturday. She hadn't thought about what would happen beyond that, if they'd still spend time together when they no longer had an excuse to do so.

Now she sensed that she wasn't the only one who had grown comfortable with this…arrangement.

"Maybe once I get through Candy's wedding this Saturday," she said.

"You don't sound like you're looking forward to it."

"I am. I mean, I want it to be a special day for my Uncle Dennis and his bride, of course."

"But?" He gave her a knowing smile. He was starting to know her quite well, or maybe he always had, she realized.

"But Candy's…a lot. She'll be occupied at the wedding, but the rehearsal dinner is another matter."

"I could come with you if you want," he said, catching her by surprise.

Unsure of where he was going with this, she said, "As a wingman?"

He shrugged. "Or...just because."

She couldn't fight off the smile, and a strange flutter filled her chest when she met his eye. "I'd like that."

13

The rehearsal dinner was less a formal rehearsal and more of a family gathering; a casual affair to prolong the celebrations, and it went without saying that it would be held in the vineyard of the Conway Orchard and Winery. Britt, the eldest of Uncle Dennis's daughters who was now running the business alongside her boyfriend Robbie, had worked closely with her sister Cora to set up the tables and plan for a tent, while Amelia and Maddie tended to the menu, deciding to close both of their establishments through the weekend for the festivities. There would be cherry pie, freshly picked from the very fields on this land, and for the main course, Amelia was offering a local white fish with farm-fresh vegetables and herbs picked straight from her garden. The wine would of course be Conway blend.

Gabby had asked her mother to deliver the bride's sample bouquet to the small stone chapel where the couple was rehearsing their ceremony. The task of arranging the centerpieces was the perfect excuse, and Candy was less inclined to argue with Gabby's mother.

Only Uncle Dennis, Candy, and the pastor would be rehearsing tonight. Given all the work the Conway women had to do to set up the dinner, Candy agreed that it didn't make sense for them to practice their walk down the aisle.

It was a small event, just the Conways tonight, and all their significant others, along with some out-of-town guests, and Candy's family members from Pine Falls. The Clark cousins and other friends would be included tomorrow for the official event.

Gabby checked her phone for any texts of complaint and was relieved to see that there were none, just a note from her mother that they'd be wrapping things up in a few minutes, and another from Doug that he was on his way.

"You're smiling," her cousin Britt observed, when Gabby stood back from the long farm table she'd been decorating.

"Oh, just relieved that Candy hasn't decided to toss her entire design scheme and go with purple instead of pink."

"And here I thought maybe you were smiling about your date this weekend." Maddie waggled her eyebrows as she carried a basket of fresh bread to the table.

My, word traveled quickly. She'd only told Candy about Doug's attendance tonight, as a courtesy. Technically, she'd had her mother mention it in passing so she could avoid Candy's reaction.

"It's not a date," she said slowly.

"A blind date," Maddie said.

"Oh, you're talking about the guy that Candy wants me to meet." Of course. Now it made sense. "I thought it was just friends and family tonight."

"Hey, the bride picked the guest list. Who did you think we were talking about?"

Gabby opened her mouth to start to explain the little arrangement that she and Doug had made with each other these past weeks, but she hadn't thought it through, and something told her that from the way her cousins were all now staring at her, there was probably little chance that they would let any excuse go without a lengthy interrogation. Even Amelia looked downright curious when she joined them with a second breadbasket, her sister Cora at her side.

"I guess I thought you meant— Well, it's sort of funny, but—"

But there was no point in saying anything because right at that moment Amelia looked over Gabby's shoulder and said, "Is that Doug Monroe?"

The rest of the girls swept their attention from Gabby to the parking lot, where one glance over her shoulder confirmed what Gabby already knew. She gave Doug a weak smile as he emerged from his car; he looked understandably shy at the sight of so many women staring at him and slowed his pace.

"So!" Maddie raised an eyebrow, not even attempting to hide her smile. "You invited Doug tonight! Here I thought you might just be bringing him tomorrow to get Candy off your back."

"That's exactly what I'm doing," Gabby insisted, even though her voice sounded as unconvincing as she felt. "You heard what Candy said about this doctor from Pine Falls. He could be anyone. And you know how I feel about blind dates and setups." She'd always been vocal about her belief that true love would find a way all on its own.

"Hey, we're only trying to fulfill your wishes," Maddie insisted. "You're always complaining about not finding anyone, so we've been trying to help."

"Although, you haven't been saying that lately," Amelia pointed out. The sisters exchanged suspicious glances, and Maddie's focus was trained on Gabby.

"No. Come to think of it, you haven't. The only guy I've heard you talk about for weeks now is your date this evening. If he's just a wingman, then why did you invite him tonight if you didn't even know that Candy had invited the doctor?"

Amelia widened her eyes and went back to the table, clearly sensing that Gabby didn't want to be pressed. She set a cheese plate down beside the bread while Britt went back into the barn to get the wine.

Gabby knew better than to think she was off the hook, not with the smug look that Maddie was giving her. Gabby looked over her shoulder, grateful to see that Doug was now chatting with Robbie and Matt Bradford, which bought her a little time to set Maddie's expectations.

"It's not a date," Gabby corrected Maddie.

"Then why bring him?"

"Candy has been trying to set me up now that you all are happily settled into relationships." Gabby thought about tonight's guest list, and how much worse it would be if Doug weren't coming.

For lots of reasons, though. Lately, she'd been looking forward to their banter, and found herself missing it when she wasn't around him. After this weekend, she'd be back to going to weddings alone, sitting at the singles table, and that thought was nothing if not very depressing.

"No explanation needed." Amelia laughed. "Candy's just so happy, she wants everyone to be happy."

Cora grinned as her boyfriend's little girl came running across the field in a white sundress. Her father, a man that Cora had been dating since the holidays, had joined the other guys now, but they all kept shooting looks over at the girls, clearly aware that something was up and it might be better to keep their distance for a few more minutes.

"It's true," Cora said, taking Georgie's hand. "She can be a little pushy, but she knows what she's talking about when it comes to love."

Gabby thought about Candy's words the other day. How she and Candy shared a lot in common, and that she understood why Gabby was holding out for the right one.

"I think you're right. And who knows," Gabby said with a shrug. "Maybe tonight is the night that I meet my perfect match."

Maddie jutted her chin over Gabby's shoulder. "Maybe you already have."

Gabby turned to see Doug walking toward her now, dressed casually in khaki pants and a linen shirt. He grinned when he caught her eye, and she felt something deep within her swell, just as it had the last time she'd seen him and the time before that.

Her cousins scurried like mice, leaving them completely alone, but Gabby stood at the table, suddenly unsure of what to say to this man who was supposed to be here to make everything less complicated.

But he just grinned that grin that crinkled his eyes at the corner and Gabby felt her shoulders relax.

"Something I said?" He raised an eyebrow and glanced at her cousins, who were now standing under various guises of looking busy when it was clear that they were blatantly eavesdropping.

She shook her head, muttering under her breath. "Let's take a walk before everyone gets here. I can give you a tour."

It was an easy excuse to break away from her cousins, even though she was rather sure they'd all be talking about her once she was out of earshot. She started with the barn where the Sunday Market was held each week from spring through fall, and then into another building, this one where the wine labels were printed and attached to each bottle.

"When my father and my Uncle Dennis took over the orchard and started making wine, they decided to name each new blend after their daughters in their life." She looked through a few of the bottles until she came to the newest one, named for Robbie's daughter Keira. "Now that Robbie and Britt are running the place, they're carrying on the tradition."

"You think Robbie and Britt will get married next?" Doug asked.

There was no doubt in Gabby's mind. "Hopefully not this year. It's still July and I have a lot of weddings ahead of me."

"Well, if you ever need a date…"

His gaze locked with hers and Gabby's mouth went dry when she considered what he meant and what might be

happening between them. But just then there was a honking of a horn, a merry sound, and one that could signal none other than Candy's grand arrival.

"I think the bride's here," she sighed, backing away. Her stomach knotted a little when she thought of how to explain Doug's presence without sparking a huge reaction from Candy, but then she wondered how she might explain it to herself. Doug was handsome, and funny, and she enjoyed his company. But he didn't want a relationship. Didn't want any of the same things she did, even if once, he'd wanted just that.

They walked outside and crunched across the gravel, around the building toward the start of the orchard, where Candy was obvious from fifty feet away, in hot pink, with a long piece of fabric roped over her arm, laughing so loudly that Gabby couldn't help but chuckle too, even though she didn't know what Candy and Uncle Dennis could be talking about from this distance.

"Look at them," she said to Doug. "They're really happy."

"They are," he said quietly.

There was something in his tone, something almost wistful, that made her turn and look at him sharply, but his attention was still on the happy couple, and now Brooke was marching at full speed toward Gabby, fire in her eyes as she spoke.

"She needed a twenty-five-foot fake train. For practice. I had to use muslin. Nearly my entire stock!"

Gabby covered her mouth to smother her laughter, but it was no use. "Oh, Brooke. I wondered what was taking you so long."

Brooke wasn't finding any of this funny. "And she has some last-minute thoughts on the bridesmaid dresses she wants to discuss before the night is through!" Brooke stared at Gabby without blinking, until she seemed to snap out of it and finally notice Doug. Now her expression turned softer and infinitely more curious. "Oh. Hello, Doug. I didn't realize you'd be here tonight."

He gave a lopsided grin and a shrug. "Kyle around?"

"Getting drinks. I need a few, as I'm sure you can imagine." Brooke motioned toward the table that was set up with wine and cider, and Doug wasted no time in dashing away in that direction.

Gabby groaned to herself as Brooke's eyes widened on hers, all talk of the demanding bride clearly forgotten.

"Beautiful night," Gabby commented, looking up at the clear sky. No threat of rain was in the forecast; she knew that Candy had a backup plan regardless.

"I'm not interested in the weather," Brooke said, linking her arm. "So, Doug, huh?"

"Oh, you know our arrangement, to be each other's wingman."

"So you said." Brooke nodded. "But you're hardly alone here."

"I am, in the sense that all of you are paired up. Well, except for Jenna," Gabby said, though they both knew that Jenna wasn't bothered too much by this. But then, Jenna was still in her twenties, and she'd dated in high school, gone to the prom, too.

Whereas Gabby had only planned it.

"Besides," Gabby added. "Candy invited my blind date tonight." She didn't add that she'd only just learned this.

Brooke looked more than a little amused. "Oh, this should be interesting."

"Maybe for you." Gabby huffed out a sigh. "I've already told her that I don't want something forced on me. I want it to happen naturally. When I meet the right man, I'll just now."

Brooke peered at her. "Will you, though?"

Gabby pressed her lips together as they neared the barn because the truth of the matter was that she didn't know how to answer that question.

"Oh! Gabby!"

Gabby closed her eyes, briefly, at the sound of Candy's trill. Brooke was quick to release her arm and scurry away to her husband, leaving Gabby alone as Candy hurried to her as best she could in her pink stilettos, her blue eyes round and excited, and her lips the exact shade of the dress.

For a moment, Gabby wondered if Candy was going to ask for changes to her bouquet, which she clutched in both hands, right at her heaving bosom, but instead, she saddled up to Gabby's side and whispered directly into her ear. "Have you seen your date for the evening yet?"

Gabby again wondered if Candy had already seen Doug, assumed something that wasn't exactly true. Not really. But now Candy was staring at the table, where people had started to sit, motioning with her eyes in a less than subtle fashion that Gabby might want to take a look.

Oh, for crying out loud.

Still, Gabby supposed that she had brought this on herself. She'd lamented her woes of being single to every female family member and friend and now they were stepping in, trying to help, and Candy...well, Candy certainly loved to help.

"I'll go over in a minute," Gabby said weakly.

Candy was nodding now, biting her lip and staring at Gabby expectantly. "You do that, hon."

Gabby felt her shoulders slump as she walked over to the table, figuring she may as well get this part of the evening over with—if only so Candy could focus on herself for the event, which she should do, considering that it was her special night.

She inched to her place setting, neatly positioned between Doug and the stranger whose back was still to her, and pulled out the chair. It caught on the grass, nearly toppling over, but a quick hand righted it.

"Thanks," Gabby said, shifting her eyes over to the owner of said hand, her heart quickening at the sight.

A handsome face. A smile that went all the way up to his hazel eyes.

"This your seat?" the man asked.

Gabby swallowed, unsure of what to say. It was her seat. And this man was handsome. And a doctor, she now recalled. But something felt off, different, and unfamiliar.

"I'm Bill, but most people still call me Billy. You must be Gabby," the man's voice was smooth, and he gave her a knowing look. "I've heard a lot about you."

Now Gabby had to laugh. Candy was prone to chronic exaggeration. "Well, don't believe everything you hear."

The man—Bill, or Billy—laughed, a hearty, gravelly laugh that pulled a smile from Gabby's mouth.

"Well, then, maybe you can set the record straight." He winked and pulled the chair out for her.

She hesitated, something pulling her attention to the left. She glanced over, expecting to see Candy, cheering with her bouquet, but instead she locked eyes with Doug.

And he didn't look happy.

*

"Will you excuse me for a moment?" Gabby didn't wait for an answer before she stood and hurried along the grass to wind her way around the table toward Doug, but it was too late. He was already setting his drink down on an over-turned barrel that was used as a tabletop, already moving in the direction of the parking lot.

She hurried in her heels, aware that her sister was staring at her, her cousins were watching, and Candy was no doubt just dying to run after her to see what was going on.

She waited until they had reached the parking lot to call out to him, even though she was sure that he was aware she was behind him. "Doug! Wait! Will you wait!"

Finally, he stopped. Pushed his hands into his pockets. Stayed with his back to her.

Her heart sank as she slowed her step, not even sure what she would say when he finally turned around. If he would even turn around.

He did. And the look in his eyes wasn't hurt or anger. It was nothing. His entire expression was flat, unreadable. And in that flicker of a second, she wanted nothing more than to see the mirth in his eyes when he looked at her. The way his entire attention once seemed to be focused on her.

Now, he struggled to make eye contact at all.

"Are you leaving?" she asked, even though that was fairly obvious.

He shrugged, glanced at her briefly. "Doesn't seem like I'm needed here anymore."

"But…" She wasn't even sure what excuse to give, or what she could say in this moment to keep him here. She wanted to say that she wanted him here, but she didn't know if that was what he wanted to hear. "But our arrangement—"

"Tonight wasn't part of the arrangement, though. Was it?" He looked at her long enough for her to drop her gaze to the ground. She kicked at a piece of gravel. She didn't know what tonight was supposed to be. She just knew that it had been nice…at first.

"Candy set that guy up with me. I told you that," she said.

He nodded, then tipped his head. "And from what I saw, you enjoyed his company."

"He caught my chair from falling," she explained. "And—"

"And he made you laugh. And you made him laugh. And he's single, handsome, and seemed more than a little interested in you."

Gabby hesitated, only because she didn't know what to say to that, or what he wanted her to say. This was the man who had made it clear that he didn't want the same things she did. Who thought weddings were expensive, frivolous parties, and that marriages could end over an argument about toothpaste.

"It's fine, Gabby."

Only it wasn't. Somewhere over these past few weeks, she'd developed feelings for him, ones that shouldn't be there, ones that would only let her down. She wanted him to stay, she wanted to talk with him through dinner. She wanted to finish giving him a tour of the land, and she wanted shared secret smiles and nudges at the expense of her matchmaking soon-to-be aunt.

But she and Doug were just friends. He'd made that part very clear.

He gave her a little smile. "I can see it's time for me to go."

"No, Doug!"

He held up a hand, stopping her. "Gabby, you know what you want. And maybe tonight you found it."

She stared at him, trying to think of what she could say, and knowing that there was nothing.

The man sitting at the table wasn't right for her—once she might have thought so, sat a little straighter, laughed a little louder, been stiff and nervous and anything but herself. And tonight, for reasons she didn't know why, but she could sense it—he wasn't the man for her.

But the man standing in front of her wasn't either.

14

Gabby finished tying the pink satin ribbon around Candy's bouquet and startled when the shop door jingled. She'd been jumpy all morning, even though she knew that it was just her mother coming in to help transfer the arrangements into the van.

"Everything okay?" Her mother was a little breathless, but her eyes were alert.

Gabby held up Candy's bouquet. It was a struggle with one hand, that much was for sure. "What do you think?"

Miriam tipped her head into a smile. "Oh. It's lovely, Gabby. But I wasn't talking about the flowers. Everything you put together is wonderful. It's you that I'm not so certain about."

Gabby sighed and carefully set the bouquet into the box with the others. "I'm fine."

Her mother didn't look convinced as she came around the counter and got to work. "You were quiet last night at the rehearsal dinner after Doug left."

Quiet, a little embarrassed, more than a little hurt. A whole lot confused. A part of her had wanted to go after Doug rather than stay at the party, but the other part of her knew that there was no sense in that. She'd gotten swept away…something that she was often accused of doing over the years.

"It's been a busy few weeks. There's nothing to talk about. I'm fine, really." Only she wasn't so sure about that anymore. Once, she'd thought that she would know the right man for her when he came along. Now, she was back to thinking that he might never show up. Or that she wouldn't recognize him if he did.

"I know you usually talk to your sisters and cousins about these things," her mother continued. "But I also know a thing or two about matters of the heart. And I know love when I see it."

Gabby held up her hands in exasperation. "Why is it that everyone else can spot love when they see it?"

"Are you telling me you didn't see the way that Doug looked at you? You were the center of his focus last night for the brief time he was there. Why, the young man practically lit up every time you spoke."

"I didn't realize you were paying that much attention to us last night," Gabby muttered. She wished she hadn't finished the bouquets so that she could keep her hands busy, make an excuse to end this conversation and stop thinking about Doug once and for all.

"Oh, I wasn't only talking about last night," Miriam said. "I was talking about all those years ago, in your debate club. The boy loved nothing more than getting your attention."

"Please." Gabby rolled her eyes, even though she was starting to wonder if it was true. She shook that thought away and began cross-checking her list to make sure that everything was accounted for and ready. "That was years and years ago."

"And last night, he never took his eyes from you. I watched him, watching you, when you spoke to that other guy."

Gabby closed her eyes and groaned. "Don't remind me."

"It was the first time I saw the light come out of his eyes when you were ever around," Miriam commented. She gave Gabby a slightly hopeful look. "I assume when he didn't come back that you weren't able to patch things up?"

Gabby shook her head and tucked the itemized list into her handbag. "No, and maybe there was nothing to patch up. Doug has made it very clear that he isn't looking for love."

Miriam just gave a little smile. "Well, looking for it and finding it are two very different things, aren't they?"

Gabby frowned, thinking of just how true that was.

She picked up one of the centerpieces. "Speaking of two people who found love when they least expected it, if we don't get these arrangements over to the reception and ceremony sites soon, Uncle Dennis and Candy won't have the wedding of their dreams."

Her mother didn't argue, and they each began carefully transporting the centerpieces to the back of the van. Gabby's mother had agreed to deliver the boutonnieres and bouquets to the bridal party, and Gabby would go to the chapel after she'd finished setting up the tent for the reception. It would be tight, but Gabby knew if she kept on schedule, she could handle it.

She brushed her hands on her apron front after she'd closed the door to the van. Her hair and makeup were already applied, and all she had to do now was quickly slip into her dress and make her way over to the lakefront.

"Well, I should get changed."

Back inside, Miriam set her hands around the large box of items for the wedding party, seeming to hesitate. "Don't you worry, Gabby. If something is meant to be, it finds a way of happening. If Doug's the one, you'll know in time."

Would she? Gabby managed a smile as she held open the door and watched her mother disappear onto the sidewalk, where tourists were milling about, mostly couples and young families; many were hand in hand.

It seemed so easy for everyone else, but then, it had also been very easy to spend time with Doug these past few weeks.

She could only hope that her mother was right. That if she and Doug were meant to be, they'd find a way. But for today, she couldn't think about her own romantic woes.

As usual, she had another person's happy ending to worry about instead.

*

Doug unloaded his groceries onto the counter of his small kitchen and heaved a sigh. He'd been back in Blue Harbor for over two months now and the boxes were still stacked in the corner of his apartment, waiting to be unpacked. It wasn't like him to be so unsettled, much less unorganized. He liked things in order. Liked to have a plan, something he could rely on, and every time he came back to this empty space it just felt temporary.

He pushed aside the nagging thought that maybe it was…maybe he hadn't bothered to set up this apartment within the first few days, let alone the first few weeks, because he knew deep down that this wasn't where he wanted to be.

Oh, he'd stay in Blue Harbor—he couldn't bear to leave it again and he had no reason to, either.

But an empty apartment was another thing. And one he'd have to get used to or at least make the best of eventually.

Right. He put his groceries away first, feeling more than a little dispassionate by the numerous frozen dinners that he had to look forward to all week unless he relied on his stack of take-out menus or learned to cook—something he could do if he wanted to learn, he was sure, but not something that interested him greatly. There was something lonely about cooking just for himself. Something affirming about his place in life.

His chosen place, he reminded himself.

He started with the books that he could quickly transfer to the shelves in the living room, and then onto the few larger boxes that held various memorabilia he'd brought with him after high school and then after college—some to be displayed, like his debate trophy, others to be set in drawers, like his Notre Dame tee shirt collection.

He moved at a steady pace, breaking down the boxes as he went, happy for the task that kept his mind off last night, and soon enough, he was on to the last of the boxes, the ones that had been doubling as a makeshift coffee table in the living room. He made a mental note to buy a proper one, and soon. Tomorrow, in fact. Once this place was furnished and complete, maybe he would feel less depressed coming back to it. Maybe he'd feel less conflicted.

The boxes were unlabeled but heavy, and he knew as soon as he popped the lid what they contained. Photos—some loose, others in frames, carefully wrapped. He'd tucked them away, out of sight, but now, he picked up the album on top—it was one that Lisa had put together after one of their trips. Like him, she was organized. Everything had its place. This was a smaller album, full of photos from one of their trips to Colorado, a ski vacation that had been a nice enough time, with good weather and a nice hotel. He flipped through the book slowly, recalling more details of the resort, the town, some of the restaurants that they'd eaten in, some more than once. In each picture they were smiling, posed, seeming happy enough unless he looked a little closer. He knew Lisa—knew her laugh and the smile that came with it, and here in the photos, her smile was frozen, like the icy winter scape behind them. And his eyes were flat, his grin halfhearted, as if he were just going along with it for the camera rather than living life.

He flipped through a few more books—one from a trip to the Caribbean where they'd snorkeled and relaxed at the beach with tropical beverages. In each one, they leaned in, but not close. And in each photo, there was a force to their poses and smiles, as if they were trying to be something they weren't.

And never could be.

He closed the box, deciding that this was one he would set in a closet, but not because it hurt too much to look back on it now.

All this time, he'd thought Lisa had broken his heart, but now, he was starting to wonder if she'd done them both a favor. If she'd been willing to admit the one thing he couldn't even to himself. They were a perfect match in so many ways, but not in the one that mattered most.

Not in the one that would keep them together. Not the one that would last. He'd left out a big factor, one that Lisa had realized sooner than him. His head was in the relationship, but his heart had never caught up.

And that, well, that was the missing piece, wasn't it?

He moved on to another box—this time his high school memorabilia that his mother had insisted he finally move out of the house now that he was back in town. He grinned as he pulled out souvenirs he'd long forgotten about—his senior class pin, his debate team medals, and a stack of four yearbooks. Of course, he'd been on the committee. He'd been active, and involved, but never popular. And truth be told, he'd been lonely, even if he'd tried to keep too busy to notice. Even his status as senior class president hadn't exactly earned him any points in the "cool" department; he'd been chosen because he was reliable and because he'd written a killer speech. Because he'd campaigned, put a plan in place, and seen it through. Because he wasn't going to accept anything but a victory. He'd wanted it on his resume. That had mattered to him a lot.

But other things mattered too. Things he'd pushed aside by keeping busy and focused on his future instead.

He'd seen how easy some of the guys had it—getting dates, going out on Saturday nights. He'd listened to Gabby talk to her sisters and cousins and friends about Chad Johnson of all people. He knew he didn't stand a chance.

Eventually, maybe he'd made sure of that.

He flipped open the first yearbook in the stack, thumbing through the pages until he reached the debate team. It was their senior yearbook, and everyone had signed it. Now, he looked for Gabby's note, even though he could probably recall it.

And there it was, in loopy purple ink: *Here's to a bright future. Something tells me that you'll find a way to get everything you ever wanted.*

He let that sink in for a long time. Thought about Lisa. The safe choice. Someone who wasn't supposed to hurt his heart, and maybe never had. Maybe, she'd just hurt his pride, made him question himself, made him wonder if he could ever really take the risk and strive for what he really wanted.

What he wanted was what his parents had. They made it look so easy, but he knew better. It had never been easy for him. Only now, he wondered if he had only himself to blame.

15

Another Saturday, another wedding, only today wasn't just any wedding. Today was Uncle Dennis and Candy's wedding, and Gabby was determined not to let anything dampen it—including her mood. The entire family would be there, and half the town, too, and Gabby wasn't going to focus on the one person who would be absent, even if her heart kept replaying last night, long after she'd returned to her empty apartment.

Nothing topped a summer wedding in Blue Harbor, at least not when it came to the centerpieces. Gabby set the last of the vases on the corner table and stepped back to make sure it didn't need any further adjustment. She smiled with satisfaction as she took in the overall feel of the tent.

Granted, it wasn't what she would choose for her own wedding—and she'd been planning that since she was only six years old. For starters, there was entirely too much pink. But then, the bride liked pink, and she wasn't shy about it either.

But Gabby preferred the understated elegance and of an all-white wedding. Or the drama of crimson red roses clutched against an ivory lace bodice. Or the whimsy of a colorful mixed bouquet, held at her side, as she walked down the aisle, barefoot…

"Earth to Gabby," a voice said from behind, causing her to jump.

She turned from the table to see her cousin Maddie staring back at her, a confection in pink chiffon ruffles.

"What are the ruffles doing on there?" She forgot her problems momentarily and stared at the new neckline of Maddie's dress.

"Last-minute change." Maddie pursed her lips and then, at the same time as Gabby, burst out laughing.

"I have a feeling Brooke didn't find this so funny."

Maddie raised an eyebrow knowingly. "You can say that again. But as they say, the customer is always right." She looked down at the dress. "And it's pretty. Just not quite as sleek as what Brooke had in mind."

"So long as it's what Candy wanted then I suppose that's all that matters, right? It's her day. And speaking of Candy, why aren't you with her?"

"I told her I'd make sure the tent looked okay." She gave a secret smile. "But the truth of it is that things were getting a little crowded at the house…"

Gabby could only shake her head. "You can help me set up the chapel if you'd like?"

"I wish I could, but I should probably get back soon. Don't need Candy worrying that something has gone wrong."

Gabby shuddered at the thought. Still, she enjoyed Maddie's company, and the truth was that she could have used the help.

"You know, hiring an assistant was the best thing I did when I opened my bakery," Maddie said, giving her a knowing look.

Gabby huffed out a breath. Being hardheaded and stubborn hadn't gotten her very far in life, had it? "I think I'll put out an ad next week."

"My! I didn't expect you to say that!" Maddie laughed.

Gabby shrugged. "What can I say? I've surprised myself recently." About a lot of things…

She began walking toward her van, which was still running, so the air-conditioning would keep the flowers looking fresh. She tried to smile, but she could feel her spirits dropping now that she was about to walk over to the chapel and get everything in order.

"Everything okay?" Maddie asked, giving her a worried look.

"Oh, fine, fine. You know me, always thinking about the flowers, wanting to be sure that everything is perfect." She supposed she had gotten off easily, with Candy not asking for last-minute changes.

"I have a feeling that nothing will ruin this day for Candy."

"It's the happiest day of her life, or so she keeps saying." Gabby smiled a little sadly now. The happiest day of her life. It was that, and not because of the flowers and the dresses, but because of the people who had all come to watch this union, to support it, and to celebrate it.

She felt her eyes mist and she had to look away before Maddie saw—a sharp cookie, that one.

Instead, she turned her attention to her cousin now that they'd reached the parking lot of the small stone chapel along the lake's shore. "Are you and your sisters okay?" She knew that they all still missed their mother, each in their own way.

Maddie gave her a little smile. "Life doesn't always go the way you thought it would, but somehow…well, somehow things still work out, you know?"

Gabby waved her cousin off and focused on the work at hand. Now, she turned off the ignition and collected the first box from the back of the van, opting to set it on the ground before closing it shut. She hadn't dropped an arrangement since her first year in business and she didn't intend to take any risks today.

No, today was a day for playing it safe. Today and maybe every day.

As Maddie had wisely pointed out, some guests did start to arrive early. Jackson was getting out of his car, and he gallantly stepped in to take the box from her arms. The gesture reminded her of Doug's equally chivalrous behavior the other night—it felt like a long time ago.

"Everything okay?" Jackson gave her a worried frown.

Gabby was starting to notice a theme to the day, and it wasn't the one that Candy had so carefully planned. She'd certainly need to adjust her demeanor before the bride showed up, which wouldn't be long now.

Gabby reached for another box, not looking to open up just now. No, better to remember that she was on the job, even if this was a family event. "Just tired. Candy's wedding has been a long time coming."

He smirked. "What on earth will she have to keep herself busy with after this?"

"Meddling in my love life, probably." Gabby adjusted the weight of the box in her arms as they walked toward the stone chapel.

"Just so long as she doesn't meddle in mine," Jackson said.

Gabby didn't bother to point out that if Candy had her way, she and Jackson would have a few "beautiful babies" together. Instead, she turned the attention off herself and said, "And how is your love life going?"

"Tourist season." His grin quirked, and she rolled her eyes dramatically as he opened the door for her.

Yep, that was Jackson for you.

"Where do you want these?" he asked, once they were inside.

"On those steps would be great," Gabby said. She knew that the procession would start from here, first with the bridesmaids, and then of course with Candy. As there was no flower girl, Gabby took the liberty of sprinkling the aisle with pink rose petals.

"Want me to save you a seat?" Jackson asked as the music from the piano began to fill the walls. Gabby looked over to see that Jenna was already seated at the bench—she must have slipped in through the side door.

Gabby nodded. "Thanks." Candy might read into it, but right now, she didn't care. Jackson was a friend and a friend he would always be.

Some people weren't meant to be anything more than that, she thought sadly.

She made a few more runs to the van, and once she was satisfied that the chapel was decorated to her liking, she stood in the vestibule, watching as the guests filtered in, checking her watch frequently. Her mother was one of the last guests to arrive, and she looked elegant in a soft blush dress.

"I rode over with your father. He and Dennis went around the side door."

It was nearly time, then. Gabby couldn't fight the wave of anticipation.

"I'd better go in. I'll save you a seat."

Gabby understood what that meant. One seat. Jenna would be accompanying the procession on piano for the duration of the ceremony, and Brooke would be sitting with Kyle, of course.

"Try to get a seat near Jackson. He's saving a seat for me." She waited for her mother's eyes to spring open, a smile to curve her mouth.

Instead, her mother nodded. "I'll look for him. He's a good friend to you, I know."

He was. But right now, Gabby's chest hurt when she thought of the other man who had been a good friend to her, but nothing more.

Gabby looked down at her phone to distract herself. She had already received three texts from Brooke. The last one was to let her know that the limo was pulling up. A moment later, Brooke came through the door, cheeks flushed, eyes a little bright.

Gabby's breath caught when she looked at her sister. "Everything okay with the dress?"

"It's perfect. I didn't change a thing, despite all her doubts, and she has waited until today to tell me it is perfect."

Gabby laughed. "Kyle came in a while ago. You'd better get to your seat before she changes her mind."

Brooke nodded and wasted no time disappearing through the double set of wooden doors.

Gabby opened them to peak a look inside, her heart swelling when she saw Jenna at the piano in a demure navy dress, looking so serious yet relaxed as she played the songs that Candy had carefully selected without missing a key. The benches were mostly filled now, and from the side door came Gabby's father, followed by Uncle Dennis.

Her heart skipped a beat as she quickly closed the door and hurried out the front door, waving to the limo until the chauffeur stepped out and came around to open the door for the women. Maddie emerged first, followed by Cora, then Amelia and Britt, who carefully helped Candy emerge without stepping on her train, which was draped over her arm.

Gabby had been hearing about this dress for weeks, all the drama and tweaks, and complaints, but now, she gasped. Her sister had done it. She had taken Candy's rather loud fashion sense and made a gown that was both dramatic yet elegant, showy but feminine. It was, to use Candy's own word, perfect.

The sisters were all helping Candy up the stairs now, and Gabby hurried back inside to double-check their bouquets. They'd walk in order of age, Maddie starting things off, Britt going last. She knew this was a complicated event for them; they all missed their mother. But today Gabby saw nothing but happiness in their eyes—a reminder that life kept going, even when it felt like the world was coming to an end.

"The procession will start after this song ends," Gabby said, catching Amelia's eye.

Her cousin reached out and squeezed her hand. "My dad's in place?"

"Looking very handsome," Gabby said, giving Candy a sly grin.

"Why do I feel nervous even though it's not even my wedding day?" Maddie suddenly asked, clutching her bouquet. "Why do I have to go first?"

"Hey, I thought you'd be happy to go first for a change. Now you see how it feels!" Britt whispered. She handed Gabby her bouquet so she could smooth the back of Candy's train. It wasn't an easy task.

After a few minutes to allow for any last-minute arrivals, the music stopped and the women all exchanged glances and excited smiles. Gabby knew that Jenna wouldn't start playing the next song until the doors were open and everyone was in position.

Gabby looked at Candy, given a silent nod, asking for consent. "Ready?"

"Honey, I've been ready since the day I knocked on that man's door."

Gabby laughed and, with a big breath, opened first one door, and then the next, careful to stand to the side where she couldn't be seen. The music started and Maddie lifted her chin and began her walk down the aisle. Cora was next.

The music was slow, but time felt slower, like it was moving at a different pace. Like somehow this moment was meant to last.

"Amelia, get ready," Gabby whispered, glancing through the space in the door hinge.

Amelia started her walk next, leaving only Britt and Candy. Gabby knew that Britt had struggled the most with the idea of a new woman in her father's life, but it was Britt who turned around and adjusted Candy's veil—because of course, Candy had a veil that would need to be lifted by her groom. Maximum drama was important to her, and they'd all ended up loving her for it.

Even Gabby.

Britt gave Candy's hand one last squeeze and then turned, took a deep breath, and walked down the aisle to her father and sisters. When she reached the end, the music would swell and—

"Gabby!" Candy hissed.

Gabby looked at Candy in alarm. Oh, no. She was afraid of this. Not something wrong with the flowers. Or the dress. Not a last-minute change. She wasn't equipped. Well, she might have a few extra roses in the van but—

"What is it?" Gabby's eyes darted to the aisle. Britt was nearly halfway down now.

"I'm sorry for setting you up last night. I saw how upset you were."

"Oh, Candy. No, it's fine!" Gabby was starting to panic. Could they really be having this conversation right now?

"I knew that Billy wasn't the one for you. I just thought that by inviting him, it might give you and Doug a little…nudge."

Ah. So it all came back to Doug. Gabby was sensing a theme. "It's fine, Candy," Gabby whispered. Her heart was beginning to race as she darted her eyes through the door again.

"You were right, Gabby. You shouldn't force love. You should just…feel it. And don't listen to those sisters of yours. When you know, you know. You just have to keep believing and have hope." She held up her bouquet, her smile so wide through her veil that Gabby could see the shine in her eyes. "I'm proof of that."

"You're a beautiful bride," Gabby said sincerely. "I'm so glad you're a part of our family."

"Just remember that when it comes time for me to plan Britt's wedding for her." Candy laughed.

Gabby frowned. "You mean?"

"Oh, you know me. I never can keep a secret. But Robbie asked Denny for her hand and…well, she's in for a surprise soon!"

Gabby smiled as she looked down the aisle to where Britt was now giving her father a kiss on the cheek, muttering some words to him, and then sliding over to stand beside her sisters.

Jenna paused, long enough to glance over at the door, where Candy stood, ever the picture of a blushing bride, in a full ballgown, clutching a ten-pound bouquet as if it were weightless, and for one brief, telling moment, Jenna's entire

face broke into a smile before she went back to her music sheet and positioned her hands over the keys.

The music swelled and the guests all stood, and Candy's smile was radiant as she began her wedding march, her twenty-five-foot train trailing behind her.

Gabby didn't rush to take her seat. Instead, she stood at the back of the room, watching from a distance, her eyes brimming with hot tears because, even though she'd said it before, this was truly the most beautiful wedding she had ever attended.

*

Gabby sipped her champagne and watched from a distance as the bridal party posed for the photographer—Uncle Dennis, Candy, and the four sisters. Their significant others hung back until they were called over to join the group that was standing along the shore of Lake Huron, the water smooth in the distance, the sky clear and blue.

"It's a beautiful wedding," a voice said behind her, and she nodded, watching as little Keira Bradford—soon to be Britt's stepdaughter now—and Cora's boyfriend's daughter shuffled to the front, near the bride. It was a sentiment that she had heard repeated many times today, and the reception had only just started. Normally, she might have taken a little credit for this, because the flowers were some of her best work, but today she knew that it wasn't about the dress or the flowers or the cake or the music. Candy's joy was contagious.

Almost enough to turn the biggest of cynics into a believer.

She frowned on that thought as she sensed the man coming to stand beside her. His suit was light grey, his tie was pink, and his eyes were full of light, and dare she say, hope.

"Doug?" Her mouth was dry. She swallowed hard, not trusting herself to say anything more until she'd figured out what exactly he was doing here. "I didn't think you were still coming."

"I can leave," he offered, even though he made no indication of doing that, much to her relief.

"No," she rushed to say. "No, please stay. You should be here. I…invited you."

He peered at her, his grin turning playful. "More like bribed me."

She laughed, if only to cover the nerves she felt, because this was unchartered territory. Up until now, she'd seen Doug as the enemy, and then, maybe as a friend. She hadn't needed to think of what she would say when she was around him—she'd just been herself.

He'd brought out the worst side of her—and the best, too.

"I'm not interrupting anything then?" He looked at her frankly, but she could tell by the look in his eyes that he already knew the answer. Maybe he just needed to hear her say it.

"Candy arranged for that guy to be there last night, as you know. And he checked a lot of boxes. But…I've started to learn that sometimes what we think we want isn't what's best for us at all."

"I'm not a doctor," he said, cocking an eyebrow.

"No, but you are an attorney," she joked.

"A divorce attorney," he reminded her.

True, all true, but she'd come around to that idea, understood his side of things. Saw that the facts weren't always as they appeared, that there was sometimes more, beneath the surface.

A lot more, she thought, looking up into his dark eyes.

"And you do like to argue," she pointed out.

He grinned as he turned to face her, his gaze traveling over her face. "Only with you, Gabby. Only with you."

"And why is that?" she asked, even though she knew. Her mother had been right. Of course. And she…she had been, so very wrong.

He gave a little shrug. "It's no fun with anyone else."

She pulled in a breath because she knew it was true. He got under her skin, he made life interesting, and he made her laugh. Made her live life to the fullest. Made her voice her passions. Made her speak her mind.

Because he wanted to hear it.

"I thought you didn't believe in all this *stuff*," she said, waving a hand at the wedding reception. The flowers, the music, the cake, the crowd. "All this romance and coupling off. I thought you didn't believe that relationships could last a lifetime."

"Ah, but that's where I have you on a technicality." He inched closer to her until she could feel the heat of his body, until he was so close that she could reach out and touch him, but she didn't, not yet, because she had to be sure. "I said I didn't believe that it could happen to me. And…I was wrong about that."

She gave him a knowing smirk, even as her heart soared. "You admit that you were wrong then?"

He pulled a face, clearly having fun with her, not that she was arguing. "Do you need me to say that you were right? Do you need to hear it?"

She thought about it for about half a second and said, "No. I'd like to think that both of us come out the winner in this situation."

"I couldn't agree more," he said softly, reaching down to take her hand.

It was warm and strong, soft yet secure. And more than anything, it felt right. So, so right.

From behind his back, he retrieved his other hand. One that held a single rose. A Juliet rose, to be precise.

"My favorite," she whispered taking it from him. She vaguely recalled telling him in passing, that first time he came into her shop. "You remembered that?"

"I pay close attention to you, Gabby. I always did. And…I always will."

"You're a good listener," she agreed. "And you're the first man who ever brought me my favorite flower. Just because."

"It won't last forever," he warned her, and sure enough, it was already starting to wilt. "But this could. You and me. What do you think?" His gaze was steady as he dropped her hand, sliding his arms around her waist instead.

She looked up into his eyes, into that devilish grin that had always stirred her up and still did. "I think," she said slowly, "that my days of sitting at the singles table have come to an end."

"Does that mean I'm going to be your plus one for every wedding this summer?"

"Only if you let me eat your cake," she said, laughing.

"It's a deal," he said, grinning widely.

"Kiss her already!" someone called out, and Gabby and Doug looked at each other in surprise before turning to see Candy watching them with obvious impatience.

"It's the bride's wish," Doug said, tipping his head. "And aren't we supposed to do everything she wants on her special day?"

Special day. It was a very special day, and not just for Candy. Because this was the day that Gabby found her happy ending, her prince charming, her rogue, and her best surprise ever.

And did she mention that kiss? The man could kiss. And when his mouth met hers as he pulled her tight against his chest, Gabby didn't even care who was watching.

Or, in the instance of Candy, cheering.

ABOUT THE AUTHOR

Olivia Miles is a *USA Today* bestselling author of feel-good women's fiction with a romantic twist. She has frequently been ranked as an Amazon Top 100 author, and her books have appeared on several bestseller lists, including Amazon charts, BookScan, and USA Today. Treasured by readers across the globe, Olivia's heartwarming stories have been translated into German, French, and Hungarian, with editions in Australia in the United Kingdom.

Olivia lives on the shore of Lake Michigan with her family.

Visit www.OliviaMilesBooks.com for more.